What Time of Night Is It?

An Ursula Nordstrom Book

Other Novels by Mary Stolz

Go And Catch A Flying Fish
Cider Days
Ferris Wheel
Cat in the Mirror
The Edge of Next Year
Lands End
Leap Before You Look
By the Highway Home
Juan
The Dragons of the Queen
A Wonderful, Terrible Time
A Love, Or a Season
The Bully of Barkham Street
Who Wants Music on Monday?
Wait for Me, Michael
A Dog on Barkham Street
And Love Replied
Hospital Zone
Pray Love, Remember
Ready or Not
The Organdy Cupcakes
The Sea Gulls Woke Me
To Tell Your Love

HARPER & ROW, PUBLISHERS
NEW YORK

Cambridge
Hagerstown
Philadelphia
San Francisco

1817

London
Mexico City
São Paulo
Sydney

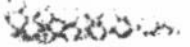

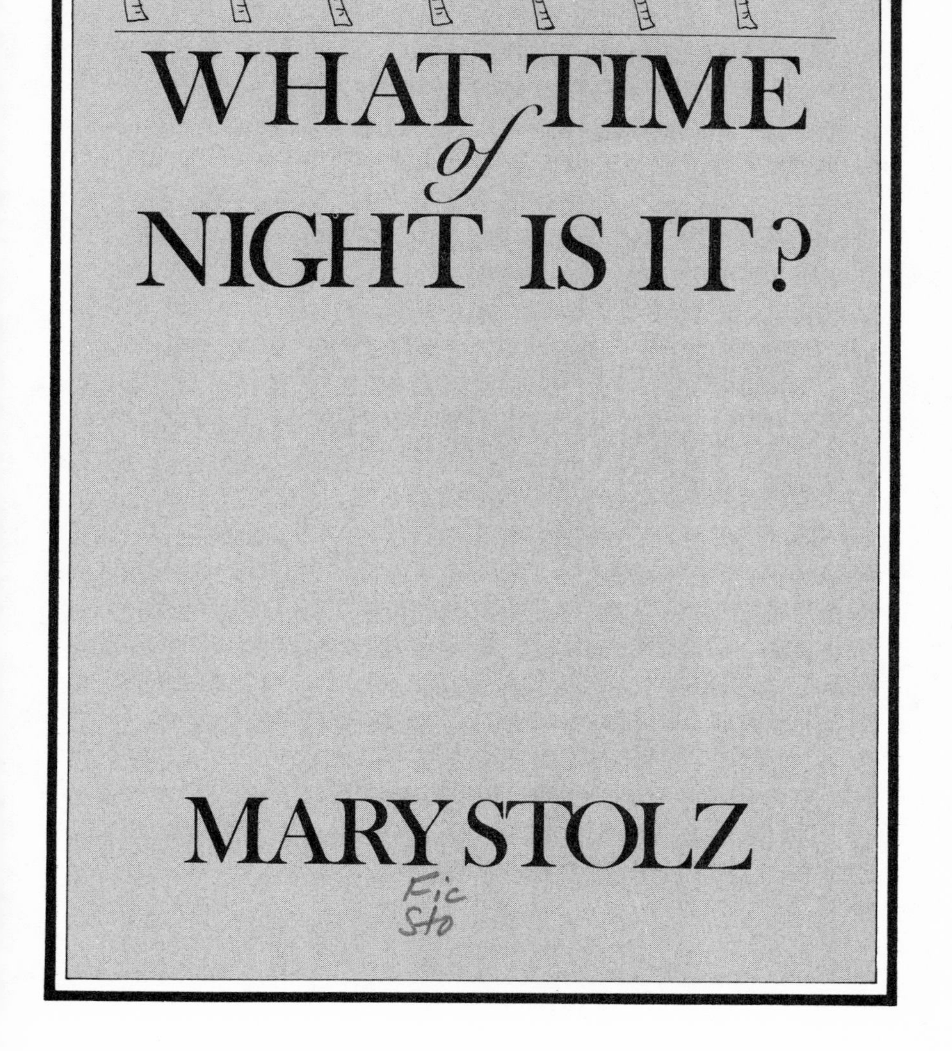
WHAT TIME of NIGHT IS IT?
MARY STOLZ
Fic
Sto

We gratefully acknowledge permission to use "Stupidity Street" by Ralph Hodgson. Reprinted with permission of Macmillan Publishing Co., Inc., from *Poems* by Ralph Hodgson. Copyright 1917 by Macmillan Publishing Co., Inc., renewed 1945 by Ralph Hodgson. Published in England under the title *Collected Poems* and used by permission of Mrs. Hodgson and Macmillan, London and Basingstoke.

What Time of Night Is It?

 Printed in the United States of America. For information address Harper & Row, Publishers, Inc., 10 East 53rd Street, New York, N.Y. 10022. Published simultaneously in Canada by Fitzhenry & Whiteside Limited, Toronto.

First Edition

Library of Congress Cataloging in Publication Data
Stolz, Mary Slattery, date
What time of night is it?

"An Ursula Nordstrom book."
SUMMARY: Examines the varying emotions and confrontations of three siblings as they attempt to rebuild a family after their mother has deserted them.
[1. Family problems—Fiction] I. Title.
PZ7.S87585Wg 1981 [Fic] 80-7917
ISBN 0-06-026061-0
ISBN 0-06-026062-9 (lib. bdg.)

TO URSULA–FOR A WONDERFUL, TERRIBLE TIME

What Time of Night Is It?

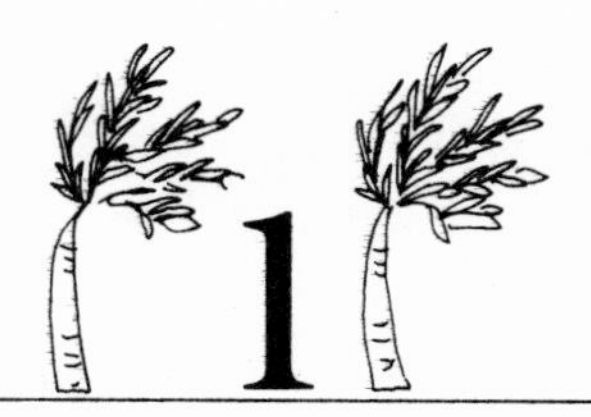

1

Taylor Reddick had never expected to be the victim of a broken home. The words were familiar. You read about, heard about, saw them—these victims. Which weren't always the children, as she saw it now. Having become such a victim, Taylor thought that Tony, her father, was maybe suffering more than even her two brothers and herself. They, at least, had friends. She had Sandy, Jem had Dan. B.J., at four, maybe didn't really need friends yet and occupied himself with the pursuit of mischief and driving her and Jem crazy. If that didn't keep him happy, it certainly kept him busy. Jem was relentlessly active. Fishing, swimming, sailing, canoeing, taking care of his aquariums, snorkeling for fish to put in them, running crab traps. He raced from one pursuit, chore, hobby—whatever his undertakings could be called—with enough diligence to send him, spent, to his rumpled bed at night. Apparently he had no trouble sleeping. Taylor had a lot of trouble sleeping. Much of Jem's busyness was shared by Dan Howard. Like Jem, ten years old. Unlike Jem, awkward and overweight. Dan was sometimes too devoted for a nature as independent as Jem's. Nevertheless, they were the best of friends. And Dan's sister, Sandy, just about Taylor's age, almost fourteen, was a steadfast presence in a tumbling world.

In the weeks since her mother had been gone, Taylor had appeared to go on doing what she'd always done. Watched birds, visited with Sandy, swum, biked, walked the beach. Things she'd have done with Junie still at home. The fact that outside you seemed to be the same as before didn't mean that you weren't gouged hollow inside. The four of them—Tony, Jem, B.J. and herself—reminded her of hermit crabs, evicted from their shells, distractedly hunting new shelter.

A broken home.

If you went by statistics—articles and polls in newspapers and magazines, interviews on television with marriage counselors and psychologists—it wasn't only possible, it was even probable that your parents' marriage would break up. Still, the words had never had anything to do with her. Like reading about cyclones in Kansas, earthquakes in Chile. You knew something terrible had happened to a lot of people, but it had nothing to do with you. And then came an earthquake, a cyclone, and tore your house down. *Your* house. *Your* home. When she had seen, on the news, pictures of stunned men and women walking over rubble in Chile, in Kansas, picking up an undamaged pot, a whole teddy bear, in the midst of devastation, she'd always wondered that they could turn to the cameras and say, as they always did, "Well, we'll just have to start over." Start over? How?

"What do they mean, start over?" she'd said to her father a couple of nights ago when they'd been looking at this scene (tornado in Texas) on their old black-and-white television set. "Their lives are smashed. Everything is wrecked. What do they mean, *start over*?"

"I guess they mean what the words say," Tony had answered. "Unless they want to cut their throats, they get to work and rebuild. It's what human beings have always done. We're the keenest destroyers and the best rebuilders on earth."

"Birds are as good. I've seen owls rebuild an osprey's nest so it was better than . . . " She'd caught her father smiling at her fondly, and faltered, tears stinging her eyes.

Tony knew lots of people, but he didn't have friends. Tony was a loner. Wouldn't a person have to feel sort of unprotected, with no friends at all?

Now, on an August afternoon, Taylor walked beside the ocean and thought about her mother. What was she doing now, this minute, that mother, that Junie? Thinking about them, the gang she'd left behind her like four passengers in a ship with a broken rudder? Did she have a notion of the wreck she'd left behind her? Well, she couldn't, or she'd have turned around and driven back the first day. Even if a woman got so she couldn't live with her husband (because of those statistics), there were still her children. She had to think about them, didn't she?

Apparently Junie didn't.

Low waves lounged shoreward, slid over wind-pleated sands, retreated almost soundlessly. Milky clouds were massed in the sky. The air was oven hot, shimmering with humidity. A pair of skimmers went by, just above the water, long lower mandibles scooping up minnows. To Taylor one of the most heart-stopping visions in life, skimmers in flight. Usually they flew in pairs, but she didn't know if they were monogamous, as some birds are. Geese. Storks. The large raptors, like eagles. Maybe birds, like people, had given up monogamy?

Well, here they were—the gang she'd left behind her. Jem apparently kept a jump ahead of his thoughts. Taylor tried to lag behind hers. B.J. was in a continual tantrum. But Tony was almost as distant, right in a room where you could see him, as Junie was in Connecticut, which was where she'd run away to. She had packed her bags in the station wagon and gone off in the afternoon, leaving a note on the coffee table that was inlaid with mother-of-pearl. That table had been one of the things they'd fought about. Tony was usually a man of few words, but about Junie's extravagance he'd had plenty to say, and all of it loud. Junie, who got her clothes at the Women's Exchange or JC Penney, who never bought stuff like linen or pots and pans, who forgot to buy her children anything to wear unless they reminded her, was bewitched by antiques. By auctions and barn sales and estate sales. She went to them with her rich friend, Bette Danziger, and spent, Tony said, like a fool. Taylor and Jem thought she found beautiful things. A set of twenty-four fruit knives and forks with gold handles. A bronze-and-marble clock that wouldn't go. A pretty bowl that they'd piled with shells and put in the center of the dining-room table. That coffee table.

And then the Chinese coromandel screen. It was a beautiful screen and had cost a thousand dollars and had caused everything to hit the fan. Tony had come out of his silence bellowing, and they'd had screaming dish-throwing battles after he'd taken the screen to an antique store to be sold on consignment. After the yelling and the smashing stopped, there'd been a simmering lull. And then there'd been Junie—gone. No more rushing into each other's arms, the way they once had done when a fight was over. This time they'd rushed apart,

Tony back into his muteness, Junie to Connecticut and a job in her uncle's office in New York City.

Taylor stopped to watch as coquinas, tiny bivalves, burrowed furiously when receding waves left them exposed on the sand. They were highly polished, exquisitely colored. Lavender, pink, yellow, green, some striped white or dark. Closely examined, the coquina was a splendid creature. Tony, who was a chef, sometimes made of them a superior pale broth, more delicate than clam broth. Birds dashed about, feasting on them. Herons, egrets, willets and dowitchers, sanderlings and knots.

Grandmother Reddick, who was coming down to see them through (how far through? Taylor wondered), wouldn't like coquina broth. Grandmother Reddick didn't like fish of any kind. She didn't like Florida, either. But she was coming, and they were grateful.

Down the beach a little way a bird alit that Taylor at first took for a heron, then realized with a jump of bliss was a black-necked stilt. There were sights granted, moments accorded, to the loving bird-watcher that drove out all feelings but joy. This was one. The stilt, shining black plumage above, chalk white below, with the slenderest neck, the thinnest, reddest legs and long yellow eye patches, stood for a moment contemplating the water, then ran zigzagging into the waves and with rapier thrust speared his fish, swallowed it and stood in momentary satisfaction, in all his beauty. Then he flew away.

Taylor watched him go, over the treetops, toward the bay, and then resumed her walk. Nice to be able to fly away. Wonderful.

Since Junie had gone, they almost hadn't seen their father. He was the night chef at a French restaurant in town, and was working extra hours because the pastry chef had hurt his back. When he was home, he slept and then took their sloop, *Loon,* out on the Gulf of Mexico for solitary sails. It had been a long time since he'd asked any of them to go with him. And it had taken him a long time to realize that she and Jem couldn't handle B.J. When he'd finally understood how desperate they were, his solution had been to send for his mother. In truth, Taylor didn't see what else he could have done. He couldn't quit his job or afford to hire someone to mount guard over B.J. So his mother was coming to Florida and they were all going tonight to meet her at the airport when her plane got in from Boston.

Grandmother Reddick had a nice neat house in Lexington, Massachusetts. Taylor had been in it once, and remembered little except a startling sense of order. Everything shone and sparkled and gleamed, though the overall feeling was one of shade and serenity. The upholstered furniture was filled with down, and without ever saying so, Grandmother Reddick gave you to understand that it would be a pity to *sink* into a chair or sofa and so disarrange its puffy outline. There were ashtrays, but even Junie had only smoked on the porch. The food, in summer, had been roasts and potatoes and vegetables cooked too much. Taylor had been nine years old on that, her only visit to Massachusetts; Jem about five; and B.J. nonexistent. They hadn't stayed long, and Taylor's chief recollection was of deep regret that they had not gone in winter instead. She had never seen snow except in movies.

It was good and kind of Grandmother Reddick to abandon, on just about no notice, her ordered and air-conditioned house, her bridge club and hairdresser, her big color television set, her calm untroubled life, to come to a house in Florida that was hot and messy, full of troubled people, that had only a black-and-white television but plenty of cockroaches. Grandmother Reddick loved television. She disliked heat, fish, roaches, irregular hours and noise.

Appreciating her sacrifice, they would do their best to welcome her. Taylor had put some hibiscus blossoms in a whelk shell on the bureau in the guest room—her grandmother's room when she was visiting and the only one with air conditioning. She'd ironed the sheets before making the bed. She'd asked Sandy for bedside reading, so *Cranford* and *The Peabody Sisters of Salem* awaited her. "Probably she's already read them," Sandy had said, "but I think rereading's almost more fun." Before leaving for the airport this evening, they'd turn on the air conditioning. Also the big wooden fan over the dining-room table, and a couple of floor fans. That might give a cool illusion.

Was it possible that Grandmother Reddick could help

them with B.J.? He was crazy about her. There was that going for them. But B.J.'s mother had left him without even saying good-bye, and his reaction had been not sorrow but rage. Rage drove him to extremes of misbehavior that even Taylor and Jem admitted were inventive. In addition to the usual dull things that any angry kid would resort to—crayoning walls, cutting fish lines, smashing things, falling to the floor in shrieking tantrums—he had a kind of stealthy originality to his mischief making. One day he'd hidden every toothbrush, hairbrush, comb, bar of soap, roll of toilet paper, tube of toothpaste, shaving cream, razor—every article he could find that anyone really needed—and none of it had ever been found. Last week he'd run away, stark naked, with his dog, Drum, as accomplice. They'd been found three miles down the key by a policeman and brought home. B.J. had been cross and unrepentant. When Tony was home, he was just sullen. In his father's absence, he was a Tasmanian devil. But just when Taylor and Jem would be about to lash him to a piling and leave him there, he'd go quiet and wistful on them, the blue eyes brimming with crystal tears. Wanting any time of truce to last as long as possible, they'd be humble with relief and accede to his any wish. B.J. was a born blackmailer, demanding Coke and cookies and late hours and constant attention, always with the threat of hysteria if what he wished were withheld.

"Little beast," Taylor said aloud. A solitary egret took wing at her voice, but went only a short way down the beach. At low tide, a great pale crescent-shaped sandbar curved out into the Gulf, providing a place for birds to rest, mingling politely at this time of year, without territorial defenses. Most of them stopped only briefly on this beach, on their way to someplace else. They could be interrupting a flight from the Alaskan tundra now, before setting out for Tierra del Fuego. So small, so tireless and powerful, and any of them had seen more of the world than she'd probably ever see. Sandy said birds made her feel provincial, they traveled such distances, so easily, to such exotic places.

"You travel a lot," Taylor had pointed out. "Greece, and Mexico and California. England that time."

"Taylor, I said *easily*. There is nothing easy about travels with my father."

2

And now, over the dunes, around a stand of sea oats, came Sandy herself, with Viva, her little Yorkshire terrier, springing beside her like a fur-bearing grasshopper.

"Do you realize that grasshoppers are just about *extinct*?" Taylor said, as they settled on the sand and dug their heels in.

Sandy peered into her canvas tote bag. It was from

the Metropolitan Museum of Art in New York City and had a print of a blue Egyptian hippopotamus on it. It was infinitely capacious and Sandy called it her life-support system. Books, candy bars, nail files, hairbrush, skin cream, tissue . . .

"With a nighty and a toothbrush," she said now, "I'd be all set to hop it without notice."

"Hop it to where?"

"That doesn't matter, Taylor, since I'm not going to, anyway. Not yet. The readiness is all."

She poked in the bag, selected a little tube of cream and rubbed the cream delicately on her nose, chin and forehead. She smelled of sandalwood soap and cucumber shampoo and was wearing an orange one-piece bathing suit that fit her like a lizard's skin. Sandy, like the rest of her family except her sister, Amanda, was overweight. Dan, at ten, looked like a fat little cop. Mr. and Mrs. Howard ran to flab. But Sandy was smooth, light footed, honey colored. She had the most beautiful complexion that Taylor had ever seen, and the best disposition.

"A person can't help wondering once in a while," Taylor muttered in a tone meant to be overheard, "if maybe it's that nothing matters enough to depress you."

"Jane Austen said about her brother that his 'Mind was not a Mind for affliction.' Neither is mine. Cheerfulness keeps breaking into my somber moods. I suppose it's a fault."

"No, it isn't. It's marvelous."

Taylor couldn't imagine Sandy slender or somber,

and would not have wanted her any way but how she was—the only sure thing in a precarious world.

"Tell me about grasshoppers," Sandy said now. "I hadn't given them any serious thought. Now that you mention it, there aren't very many. Not around here. I suppose there are still some inland."

"Tony says when he was a boy in New England, summers used to flutter and glow—"

"That's nicely put."

"Butterflies, fireflies, ladybugs, grasshoppers. We don't see things like that. Tiny, *scant* examples, but nothing like Tony's summers. Fluttering and glowing. No wonder the birds are disappearing. There's nothing for them to eat. They spray for mosquitoes and kill everything but."

"Shore birds seem to be okay."

"Oh, Sandy—they *aren't.* The brown pelican is endangered, the— Everything alive is endangered. Except human beings."

"Why do you except us? Seems to me we're in plenty of danger. From ourselves, of course, but just the same."

"People are survivors. Let every other living creature perish—we'll outlast them."

"You could be wrong. Even if you aren't, you should be thinking positive things in the meantime. Plan on something you'll adore. Plan a trip to the Galápagos Islands, where you will be able to see with your very own eyes the tool-using sparrow."

"Finch."

"Finch. Maybe I'll go with you."

"Actually, I wasn't thinking about birds."

"Your mind was a total blank?"

"Don't, Sandy."

"Sorry. But after all. You were stumping along, staring out to sea with that daft expression you get when you're thinking about owls or eagles and whether they'll survive the human race—"

"They won't."

Sandy rummaged in her bag. "Want a granola bar?"

"No, thanks."

"Hand cream? Nail file? A good book?"

"Not now. What are you reading?"

Lately Sandy had been into female novelists heavy on sex and obscenities. She covered the books with innocent-appearing jackets to fool her parents, who were easily fooled. Louisa May Alcott wrapped around the steamy prose of Kate Millett. *Jane Eyre* enfolding Erica Jong. Now she took out a paperback edition of *Gone with the Wind* and patted it fondly.

"Are you gluing your jackets on now?" Taylor asked.

"This is the real thing. I need a respite from carnality. The last one had everything but pop-up parts. Now, *this* is a scrunchy book." Sandy called a book scrunchy when it so absorbed her that no request, demand, entreaty could reach her, when she came out of the printed world into the real unwillingly and always at her own pace. "Kind of prefeminist, mind," she went on, "but just great. You can have it when I'm through. It'll do you good."

"Thanks, but I saw the movie."

"Taylor! That's *not* the same. You *have* to start reading something in addition to the Audubon monthly and Roger Tory Peterson."

"Okay, okay—"

Book addicted in a book-ignoring society, Sandy insisted on lending books to people who hadn't asked to borrow them. She'd left *Treasure Island, The Once and Future King* and *The Yearling* for Jem. Therein, she said, lay the cure for his recent and abnormal condition of edginess. Taylor thought a six-month survival course for B.J., maybe in Alaska, would be a better remedy.

"They give me perspective, my books," Sandy was going on. "You and Jem don't know what you're depriving yourselves of. Has he read anything I left for him?"

"Not that I've noticed."

"Well, *you* could. What about *Catcher in the Rye*? Have you started it?"

"Sandy, stop nagging."

"For instance, if I didn't read widely, I might actually think I was the only girl in the world whose mother spikes her morning juice with vodka. And I might think that those Victorian fathers with their life-and-death throathold on their families had actually died out with Victoria, instead of being reincarnated to smash the spirits out of twentieth-century victims."

"If your spirit is smashed, I'm getting out of the way when a whole one comes along."

"I was thinking of the rest of them. Dan and Amanda. Mostly my mother."

Taylor, who spent a lot of time at the Howards', understood. If Mrs. Howard started out of a room, her husband would say, "Where are you going?" If she went toward the telephone, he'd ask who she was going to call. If she'd just hung up, he'd ask who was that. He expected the morning mail to lie untouched on a table in the foyer until he got to it in the evening. Sandy and Amanda paid no attention to that rule, and Dan never got any mail, but Mrs. Howard scrupulously waited to be handed any correspondence that was for her and then submitted to a quiz about its contents. Mr. Howard often said he lived for his family, and Taylor thought he was telling the truth, since except for Sandy they certainly were not allowed to live for themselves. He showered them with unrelenting affection and was subject to fussy rages at signals of opposition. "He calls it love and I call it persecution," Sandy said now. "There was some American general in the Vietnam war who said they had to destroy a village in order to save it. Apparently he thought he was making sense. From what I've read, apparently a whole lot of Americans thought so too. That's how my old man's head works. He's destroying us in order to save us."

"From what?"

"That's the question. Since what we really need saving from is him. There are Dan and Amanda at the shrink every week, and my mother clear around the corner from booze. I've considered killing him, but I'm afraid I'd get caught."

"How come he isn't destroying you?"

"I'm insensitive."

"You are not. That's a dumb thing to say."

"No, it isn't. I am. In my opinion the worst curse that can be laid on a person is a thin skin. I have a positively calcareous covering. That means shell-like."

"I know what it means. Don't you *ever* worry, Sandy? I don't mean just about your family. About the world. What's going to happen to it. Bombs all over the place and the ozone layer disappearing and everybody fighting and hating everybody else. What can all that *come* to?"

"Armageddon, I expect."

"That doesn't worry you?"

"It scares me, if that's what you mean. But Taylor, just exactly what are we—ordinary people who aren't even of age yet—going to do about it?"

"Nothing. There's nothing we can do. It's all too big. And I guess too far along—toward Armageddon."

"So what's the point in worrying?"

"If there's one thing I know about worry, it's that there does *not* have to be any point. You just do it, if you're the worrying kind. I'm that kind."

"You're miserable about Junie. Of course you are. But putting aside the fate of the world, Taylor, and getting down just to us, I think it's better to live in a house divided than in one that's crumbling to bits around you."

Was it asking too much to want a house neither divided nor crumbling? Look at Chrissie Dobkin and her family. Nothing awful ever happened to them. Junie thought that having a baby every year, the way Mrs.

Dobkin did, was awful. But the Dobkins stayed together, and the Dobkins seemed happy.

"Do you think Chrissie and her family are really as happy as they seem?" she asked Sandy.

"I'd love to say I didn't. I mean, it's really weird, all that harmony. But I guess they are. There's never any evidence to the contrary." She put *Gone with the Wind* back in her tote bag, got out the granola bar. "Sure you don't want half? Okay." She peeled the wrapper and started munching. "Amanda's letting her hair grow. It's driving the old man bananas."

"I knew she'd get tired of that poodle cut. Why shouldn't she let it grow?"

"Not on her head. On her legs and under her arms. She says shaved legs and armpits are a sign of a male-dominated woman. Alexander agrees with her."

It was a wonder to both of them that Amanda, who faced her world with a sullen expression, as if sure some nasty turn of events was overdue, had at last, at age sixteen, managed to get herself a boyfriend. All her life her father had kept her on a choke collar, as he kept Dan and his wife and the employees at the three or four banks he owned. He did not consider that Amanda was old enough or sufficiently responsible to "begin keeping company." "Except, of course," he would say, "at parties, gatherings." He did not appear to notice that Amanda was never invited to parties or "gatherings." From the time she'd been little, Amanda had been one of those people just naturally excluded. "And for no reason anyone can *see*," Sandy would remark from time to time with concern. "She'd be pretty, if she didn't look like the end of hope and joy all the time, and she's got a nice figure, if she'd just straighten up. She's awfully bright. So I don't know what's the problem."

Taylor thought that it wasn't so much that people didn't like Amanda as that they didn't notice her. She seemed to be completely overlookable and forgettable, except by her father, always training that furious concentration on her.

Amanda, a vegetarian, took her meals apart from the family. At the beginning of her vegetarian period she'd eaten in the kitchen, but she had recently started carrying meals up to her room. Mr. Howard bore with this as a caprice that would pass. So long as she was where she could be found, he gave her her head, and did not think to supervise her expeditions to the Sprout Spout, where she purchased natural foods. There, over a bin of sun-dried unsulphured apricots, she'd met Alexander, and she'd fought for him. She'd threatened to run away, to commit suicide, to go on the streets, if deprived of him. Mr. Howard sent her to a psychiatrist (who said let her keep Alexander) and had an undercover investigation made into Alexander's background. Uncovered, it turned out to be as correct and reactionary as even Mr. Howard could have wished. Alexander was rejecting his upper-middle-class background by going bearded, beaded, and bathless. Sandy said her father had degraded them by this FBI snoopage. "But then, just by existing, my father degrades us." "What do you think of Alexander?" Taylor had asked and Sandy had shrugged. "Smells a bit high. Still, he's coaxed the first real smile out of Amanda since she got that pony on her tenth birthday. The one she fell off of, so Dad took it away from her. I think this is the summer of Alexander's repudiation of his parents' values. He's going to Princeton in the fall and doesn't show any signs of rejecting that."

Finishing off the granola bar, Sandy regarded her own legs and then Taylor's. Satin smooth and hairless.

"I've got some hair under my arms," she said. "And on the Mound of Venus, of course."

"The what?"

"That's what they call it. It isn't in Webster Two, but it's been in some of my books. Mound of Venus. Sounds so classical. Someday when somebody's making love to me I plan to whisper that in his ear—it'll give the affair tone, don't you think?"

"Should," Taylor said absently.

"Do you ever think about it? Being made love to?"

"Right now I'm thinking about my grandmother."

"Ah. Well. Okay, let's talk about your grandmother."

"We're all driving to the airport to meet her tonight."

"Making you nervous, huh?"

"Oh, boy. I mean, it's awfully kind of her, to come on such short notice—"

"You've said that, by my count, ten times a day for the last week, and that's not counting when I'm not with you."

"I just know the heat is going to be too much for her. Her letters to Tony in the summer are practically only about how hot it is. And that's Massachusetts. New England. How hot can it get up there?"

"Have you noticed that hot summers don't keep people away anymore? Remember when Florida just about emptied out, come July or August? Now look."

Even on so scorching a day, the beach was crowded. Not like the east coast. But still. A few years ago, Taylor thought, you could have come over here on such an afternoon and found nothing but birds. Now, all year round, tourists, retired people, aimless young people (riffraff, Mr. Howard called them) found their way to Florida. She wondered if even the tourists ever went back where they came from.

"Do you suppose there's anyplace left in the world where you could live without seeing people?" she asked Sandy. "Some desert island, miraculously overlooked. I wonder if Jem and I could find it."

"I hope not. I'd miss you terribly."

"You're invited."

"I wouldn't go to a desert island unless it had a public library on it."

Taylor laughed, getting to her feet and brushing sand from her bottom. "I better get home and think what to have for dinner."

"You don't know yet?" Sandy was always keenly interested in the Reddick menus. At the Howards', they ate well or indifferently according to the cook of the moment. No cook stayed there long, and once Mr. Howard had tried to hire Tony away from L'Auberge Jean-Jacques. His proposal had arrived by mail in a patronizingly worded letter that Junie and Tony had had a lot of fun responding to in a properly pompous way. There'd been a time when her parents had had fun together that way, other ways. Not in all ways, of course, but who'd expect that?

"I don't even know if it's my night to cook or Jem's," she said to Sandy.

"Yours. Because three nights ago when I had dinner with you, Jem got it. Lovely." She sighed. "Those parmesan popovers!"

"See you."

Walking up the beach to where she'd left her bicycle lying on the sand, Taylor wondered if it had been possible that Junie *had* wanted to have fun in all ways at all times? Taylor wasn't quite fourteen, but she'd been aware for years that such a state of things was impossible. Surely her mother, at her age, should have known too? Or not? Who knew what they knew or why they did the things they did?

She pedaled through the sun-drugged, nearly empty streets to the other side of the island and home.

3

The place beside the house where their father usually parked his Volkswagen was empty, but Taylor found her brothers home. They were fishing off the dock that ran from their house out into the bay.

Our house, she thought, trying to see it through her grandmother's eyes. Would Grandmother Reddick ever see it as beautiful? Had she ever? An old Florida house of weathered cypress, ten acres of trees and mangroves and mud flats surrounding it.

Strewn along the outdoor porch were sails, oars, tackle boxes, gaff nets and mullet nets, crab traps and brightly painted buoys. Life belts, fishing rods, picnic hampers. Gasoline containers for the skiff tied up to a piling halfway down the dock. Some old chairs. A chaise no longer limber enough to be moved from one position to another. A round wooden table. All had known so much of the elements that they looked like driftwood somehow formed to human usage. Jem and Taylor had tidied up indoors, but nobody ever bothered with the porch and the dock. Should we have? Taylor wondered. Too late now.

Drum, B.J.'s dog, lay under the house on the cool wet sand. Tut, their cat, who fancied Jem above the rest of them, sat beside him, no doubt hoping for a fish-head snack.

"Where's Tony?" she asked Jem.

"Dunno."

"Do you know, B.J.?"

"Somewhere. Jem got a snook!" he said excitedly.

"In the afternoon?" said Taylor, glancing over at the bridge where several fishermen were tending their poles and nets, with a clear view of this house and dock. "Did they see you?"

"Don't think so. I gigged him this side of the dock and sort of worked him ashore underwater. He's a big one. All filleted and in the fridge. We can have him for dinner tonight. Maybe be our last chance at fish for ages."

Snook, a game fish, was by law only to be caught with hook and line, but Tony and Jem and other people in the village now and then gigged one that practically asked for it, lazily swimming within reach. Taylor didn't approve, but you couldn't say anything to Tony or Jem. They did what they wanted to do, and they both loved snook. So, for that matter, did she.

"Stop frowning at me," Jem said. "You'll eat it, you know."

"I know. But maybe Amanda's got the right idea, being a vegetarian."

"Suit yourself. I'll stop eating fish when the ocean runs out of them. With their goddam oil slicks, that may be pretty soon. You know that saying, *O Lord, thy sea is so large and my ship is so small*? If that's the case, how come they keep bumping into each other all the time? There's another couple of goddam oil tankers collided off the coast of France."

"You're going to have to stop swearing. Grandmother Reddick doesn't like it."

"Let her tell me, okay?"

Refusing to discuss oil spills with Jem didn't mean she didn't care about them. She cared. She *dreamed* of fish suffocating, birds dragged down to drowning by oil on their feathers, the winter home of the whooping cranes made viscous and unlivable over there in Texas by the uncapped oil pouring up from Campeche, Mexico. Why *did* those goddam tankers collide when they had all the ocean to maneuver in? Yet they did, over and over. Beaches and seas all over the world became sepulchers for wild things that could not defend themselves.

"Hateful, hateful," she said under her breath, but Jem heard her.

"What's hateful?" he asked, reeling his line in. Some smart fish had neatly removed the bait, and Jem patiently rebaited the hook with a squirming pinfish. Taylor had to look away.

"Lots of things are," she said. She sat down beside him. "It's just that I think if people gig snook illegally and think that's all right, it's just one fish and who cares, then other people will think it's all right to kill hawks. Or eagles. It's a *principle,* Jem."

"So, in principle I agree. But guys are going to go on killing as long as they can get away with it. Some guys just plain like to kill things, *especially* if they aren't supposed to. I figure so much goes on in Florida that's illegal, what difference does a snook here or there matter? At least we eat what I go after. Those dudes firing away at hawks aren't going to *eat* them."

"Oh, don't."

"You started it."

"All I said was you shouldn't gig in broad daylight, with people on the bridge where they can see."

"Okay, you've said it. But is that principle? Sounds more like caution to me."

"It's just that—"

"Taylor, will you pipe down? All you do anymore is

tell me and B.J. what we shouldn't do. Can't gig, can't swear. I'm sick of it."

"It's just that Grandmother Reddick—"

"Taylor! Jeez. You've got B.J. here thinking she's the witch of the woods."

"I do not think Granny's the witch of the woods," said B. J. His sister and brother looked at him in surprise. "Granny?" said Taylor, and B.J. replied calmly that that was what other children called their grandmothers. "Granny," he repeated, sounding pleased. "*She* won't take me somewhere and then go away and forget me."

Taylor and Jem exchanged a look of dismay. Who told him about it? Taylor wondered. How had he found out about that long-ago and apparently forgotten day? The recollection had been lying there in his mind all along, not referred to by B.J. but coiled all this time in his memory like a worm in the salad? Someone, carelessly, had spoken of it and he had overheard? Taylor could easily imagine Junie, talking in the living room with one of her friends, or over the telephone, telling the story ruefully, not sparing herself, but not, either, remorseful. After all, nothing terrible had come of it. Something awful *might* have happened, but hadn't, and Junie spent no time on guilt or regret. "If you've done something you regret, be sorry and then forget it. If you have to apologize to somebody, do that, and then forget it." That was Junie's position.

"Isn't that too easy?" Taylor had said doubtfully.

"Not for me."

Taylor had not known then and did not know now if her mother really meant that, or just wanted to mean it because she so disliked ill feeling, reproaches, recriminations. Junie wanted people to be happy. Failing the real thing, she thought it common decency to pretend. How, oh how had she and Tony ever thought to make a union that would last? How had they managed to make it last as long as they had? Tony couldn't *pretend* anything, and joy was hardly second nature to him. Of course, if they hadn't made such a colossal error, she and Jem and B.J. would not now be sitting on the dock, products of a bust-up.

One day, when B.J. had been about two years old, his mother had tossed him in the car and driven off to a nearby shopping mall to buy, as she said later, a cheap little terry robe as her old one had disappeared. Jem and Taylor supposed that she'd left it somewhere, on the beach, over on Wrasse Island. Someplace. Junie lost her possessions with regularity but as she wore next to nothing and didn't care what anything looked like anyway, losing a shirt or a robe or a pair of scuffs was no big deal.

That day she'd gone to the mall, B.J. beside her in the station wagon, to get herself a terry robe, and she'd come home without him.

Taylor, hearing the wagon on the shell driveway, had gone out to meet her mother. She'd looked in the car, asked her mother curiously, "Where's B.J.?"

Junie's hand flew to her mouth. "Oh, my god, Taylor. I had him with me, didn't I?"

"Are you crazy?" Taylor shrieked. "Of course you had him with you! You—"

"Get in," Junie ordered.

"But—"

"I said *get in.* Now."

Taylor jumped into the front seat and Junie tore up the driveway onto the road without looking. She crossed the bridge at a speed that caused fishermen, who were always lined up there, to turn and glare. Junie didn't see them.

"I can't understand it," she said to Taylor as they sped along. "Grub around in my bag there, Taylor, and find me a cigarette. No, no . . . *light* it for me."

"But—"

"Are you trying to torment me? Light the cigarette, will you? Thanks. Thanks, honey. No, but I just do not understand what I could've been thinking of . . ."

Not about B.J. anyway, thought Taylor. She was frightened, partly at the way her mother was driving, but mostly at the thought of losing B.J. People kidnapped children, didn't they? Not for money, but because they were so adorable. People who didn't have children of their own but craved them. And B.J. was so friendly, so beautiful, so trusting. He'd go with anybody. And then what? Would the people who took him love him, or would his little body be found, the way little bodies were found—

"Taylor, stop crying," Junie said. "You'll see. He'll be fine."

"Fine! You don't even know where he is!"

"I left him in that toddler pit. You know, where they have slides and teeter-totters and jungle gyms—all that stuff tarted up like tenth-rate Disney, as if there was first-rate Disney—and he was adoring it. Everybody leaves their kids in that pit while they just go to a nearby store—all I wanted was to get the damn terry robe and have a cigarette in *peace.* He'd been whining all day. That's why I went really, to give him a change, get him to *stop whining.* You were like that, you know, at his age. Not Jem. But you were, *and* a grabber. Try to wheel you in the supermarket and the only safe track was dead center in the aisles. Get close to the shelves and you'd bring down a whole cracker section. *Or* something with bottles. Nice lot of broken pickle jars once. I won't forget that. You know, Taylor, I think children of two should be put painlessly to sleep and then awakened with a kiss at about age ten. Like beautiful butterflies, they'd—they'd—emerge . . ." She'd had to stop talking. Tears ran down her face and the cigarette fell to the floor, still burning. Taylor ground it out in the ashtray and sat hugging her arms close, swallowing hard, sweating, chilly, and much too frightened to talk. Junie said three or four times that they'd see, he'd be fine, but Taylor couldn't give her mother the reassurance she was looking for. She was wondering if they'd ever see B.J. again.

They found him. There he was, in the toddler pit, sliding down something shaped like an alligator with a trough in its back. He was laughing, having a wonderful time. It was obvious that he had no idea that he had been, for a little while, an abandoned, a forgotten child.

Junie sat on a bench and closed her eyes. "Get him, Taylor," she said in a trembling voice. "Get him for me, will you?"

They were quiet on the way home, except for B.J., who hummed in the back seat. At home, when he'd gone to look for Drum, Taylor said to her mother, "Are you going to tell Tony? Because if you don't want to—"

"Of course I'm going to tell him. I don't keep things from your father."

"But this was so . . ." Taylor stopped.

"So *what*?"

"Well—awful. I think."

"It *might* have been awful," Junie said sharply. "I might have had to kill myself. But the fact is, nothing happened at all. There he is, prancing around with Drum, not a care in the world. So what am I supposed to do? Grind my face in the shells? Have a nervous breakdown? What do you suggest, Taylor?"

"I don't know," Taylor said in a thin cold voice. She was not over her fright. She'd get over it, of course. But not as easily as Junie had got over hers. Never that easily.

In the evening, after B.J. had gone to bed, Junie told Tony and Jem what had happened. Jem took his mother's position, that since nothing had happened, there was no big deal. But Tony, paling under his tan, had got up and walked to the end of the dock and sat there for a long time in the dark. Taylor and Jem had gone to their rooms, he to the one he shared on the ground floor with B.J., she to her octagonal tower at the top of the house. Afterward, for several days, Junie's laughter had had a sort of brittle chime, and Tony had been even quieter than usual.

But time went by and the matter was forgotten. Well, Taylor thought now, of course it wasn't forgotten. Just sunk beneath the surface like something weighted and tossed in the bay. How had B.J. found out? Some chance conversation on Junie's part? None of the rest of them would have mentioned it. Taylor and Tony because it could touch them still with anxiety. Jem because he didn't think it was important. Or had B.J. not, after all, been asleep that first night? Had he stood in the shadows in the hall and listened to his mother admit she'd taken him out and then *forgotten she had him with her*?

Taylor turned and put her arms around her little brother and held him tight, kissing his silky hair. For a moment he yielded against her, then squirmed and pulled away.

Fifteen minutes later, when she came down from her room, she grabbed his shoulders and shook him till his head wobbled.

"You poisonous little *toad*," she yelled. "I *told* you to stay out of my room! I'll brain you—"

"Hey!" Jem shouted, pulling B.J. out of her grip. "What the heck are you doing? Are you crazy?"

"He glued the pages of my bird book together! He's *ruined* it and I hate him!"

"Your field guide? For gosh sake, Taylor," Jem said

in disgust. "You'd think he'd brought down the last American bald eagle with a slingshot. Tony'll get you another guide—"

"You don't understand anything," Taylor said, half sobbing. "I've had that book since I was six. It's got all my markings in it. It's—it's worn and handled and shows I've been watching birds for years—"

"Shows *who*?"

"Shows—shows nobody. Shows *me*. It's my book, it's—part of *me*. Oh, you just don't understand—"

"Maybe I do," Jem admitted. "Can we unstick the pages?"

"No. We can't. It's ruined forever."

During this conversation, B.J. had been looking speculatively from his brother to his sister. "Taylor," he said, "I'm sorry I did that."

She rounded on him angrily. But there he stood. Small. Deserted. With that baby-blue expression.

"It's okay," she said, wiping her eyes. "I don't think you know what you're doing half the time. I hope you don't," she muttered.

"Do you hate me?"

"Of course I don't hate you. I love you."

"You said you hated me."

"People say things. When they're angry. You get people angry."

"I know," he said softly, and Jem and Taylor gave each other a hopeless look.

"Grandmother can't get here too soon to suit me," Jem said, reeling his line in again. Twisting on the hook was a small sea trout, the kind he ordinarily threw back. This one he handed wriggling to B.J. "Go feed your heron, okay?"

B.J. started carefully down the dock toward a big blue heron who always arrived when they started fishing. B.J. and Jem called him Benjamin. Now, holding out the fish, B.J. approached the bird that was taller than he was. Benjamin, on his stalky legs, moved forward slowly, stretched his long neck out, took the trout in a flashy grab, retreated a few steps and gulped it down. Then he drew up one leg and appeared to study B.J., who stood very still, eyeing him back.

"Look at that, will you?" Jem said, laughing. B.J. had pulled up his right leg and stood, balancing without difficulty, facing his friend. "Boy, once in a while I wish we had a camera."

Doesn't she miss us? Taylor thought. Wouldn't she want to *see* something like that? "I'll never understand," she said softly.

"So why go on trying?"

"You sound like Sandy."

"Maybe we're right. Ever think of that? If you can't understand something, what's the point in trying to understand it? You don't eat, Taylor. You don't sleep. It's just dumb."

"How do you know I don't sleep?"

"I hear you prowling in the night. I don't sleep so great either."

"Then you are . . ." She stopped.

"Are what?"

"How do I know, Jem? Upset, nervous, angry—how do I know? But you go around pretending nothing's wrong, and I think it's rotten of you."

"You want me to go around moping, like Tony?"

"Don't you dare say anything against Tony!"

"I'm not saying anything against him," Jem explained patiently. "I'm saying how he is. And he is. Looks like he's on his way to a funeral most of the time."

"I'm not going to talk to you anymore."

"Suit yourself."

Taylor stamped down the dock, causing Benjamin to let out a hoarse squawk and take flight, a flappy awkward flight at first that turned into easy soaring.

"Now look what you've done!" B.J. shouted angrily. "You made him fly away!"

"Why shouldn't he fly away?" Taylor yelled back. "That's the *fashion* around here, flying away!" She tried to bang the screen door, but it wouldn't, so she pulled it shut, went into the living room and sat on the floor, leaning against the sofa, out of breath as if she'd been running.

Benjamin. Why not Beatrice? Men, she thought. Boys. Everything in their image. Everything their way. She recalled Junie's saying once that they were the only two females in the house. Everything else, including the pets, was male. Now I'm the only one, she thought. Well, after tonight there'd be Grandmother Reddick. She did not think she and her father's mother would be forming a consciousness-raising group of two. There was no question in Grandmother Reddick's mind that the world had been made for men and ought to be run by them. "Not that I'm prejudiced," she'd say, "but I simply could never go to a woman doctor or lawyer. I just wouldn't be comfortable." Probably, if she was here long enough, she'd raise another little male chauvinist in B.J.

Down the shell driveway into the turnaround came her father's Volkswagen. You'd think because of its cute shape and perky name, Beetle, that a VW could not contrive to sound morose, but Tony's car seemed to plod down the drive, projecting dejection. Taylor got up, went over and peered through the window. Her father was sitting motionless behind the wheel. He did that all the time now. Arrived home and then sat for a while, as if trying to collect the bits of his broken self. So he can face us, she thought. The children he doesn't know what to do about.

I wish we were older, she thought. I wish Junie had waited to run away until we were all older.

4

A loudspeaker announced that Eastern Flight 109 from Boston and Tampa was landing at Gate Four.

"Okay, kids," said Tony. "That's us."

Taylor, who'd been toying with the notion of a plane crash, stood and followed her brothers and her father out of the coffee shop.

Her vision blurred and a belt of anxiety tightened around her chest as she watched the huge plane taxi to a stop.

Nothing is ever going to be the same again, she thought. When the engine on that plane stops, our old life stops. Tony says it's just for a while, just till we get running on an even keel. "Mother hates Florida. She'll only stay for a while, to get us on the right track." That's what Tony had said, out of B.J.'s hearing, trying to reassure Jem and Taylor. He knows we don't want her, and he knows we can't do without her. And I didn't really wish the airplane would fall down. Grandmother Reddick had a perfect right to stay alive. And the other people on Flight 109. She hadn't wanted it to crash. She'd just thought, she supposed, that if some plane somewhere *had* to crash this evening, why shouldn't it be—

"What's the matter, Taylor?" her father asked.

"Nothing's the matter."

Tony said the arrangement with his mother would just be for a little while, but Taylor knew, the way you sometimes *know* things (like when somebody isn't going to answer the telephone and you know from the first ring that this time there isn't anybody home), that Grandmother Reddick, now walking into the baggage waiting room, was with them for good.

Just between the steps of the plane and this large room where in a few moments luggage would begin to trundle past on a revolving rubber carrier, Grandmother Reddick's face had begun to be lightly dappled with sweat.

After she'd greeted them, and without detaching

B.J., who clung to her thigh, which had to be sort of heating, she said to Tony, "I will never understand how a man born and brought up in New England can tolerate this *intolerable* heat. It's a furnace at nine in the evening!"

"Tell you what, Mother. Why don't you go into the airport building with the kids, and I'll wait for your bags?"

"How, pray, are you going to know which bags are mine? Really, Tony." She patted B.J.'s back. "How's my little love been keeping?" She and B.J. had a good thing going between them and always had had. Which is the only thing going for us now, thought Taylor.

Tony was studying the luggage belt with frowning concentration, though as his mother had pointed out he wouldn't know which bags to fall upon when they sailed toward him. Jem was standing a little to one side of his grandmother, Taylor a bit on the other side. Silence enveloped their small party while all around them the excited greetings common to a Florida airport took place. People from the north coming with their children to visit retired grandparents. Babies born and grown to traveling age now were thrust into waiting grandparental arms, amid cries of "Oh, you darling, oh precious, you just come to Grandma! How he does favor you, Johnny, oh my goodness, I can't believe I'm holding him at last!" Yankees who'd found it much less expensive to vacation on the beaches in summertime now stood grinning at relatives about to be blessed with their company, or went off to arrange for rental cars. It was a cheerful commotion. A good deal of comment on the heat and humidity, of course. But only Grandmother Reddick seemed to be already desperate about it.

"There they are, Tony. The navy ones with red pompoms." She took a handkerchief from her bag, patted her brow and the back of her neck. Removing her glasses, she rubbed her eyes, then stood a moment, blinking as if perplexed. For that moment, she looked so unfamiliar and so uneasy that Taylor felt a rush of pity.

"Is that all you brought?" Tony asked. "Two bags?"

"I have a small trunk packed and ready to ship down. My neighbor, Mr. Mills, said he'd take care of it. If it should prove necessary."

Boy, what a mess, Taylor thought. She doesn't want to be here. We don't want her here. And it's all Junie and Tony's fault. People should have to study, and then take written and oral exams, and then psychological tests and get licenses, before they were *allowed* to get married and have children. . . .

They went to the parking lot, B.J. chattering, jumping up and down, asking his grandmother if she'd read to him as soon as they got home, if she'd play Go Fish, if she'd sleep with him.

"Sleep with you! My goodness, I should think not, B.J. A big boy like you—"

"But Granny, I want you to!"

Grandmother Reddick stopped walking, stared down at her small grandson. Her mouth framed a question she didn't ask.

"He says that's what all children call their grandmothers, and that's what he wants to call you," Jem explained.

A smile—really a sweet smile, Taylor thought—touched Grandmother Reddick's rather thin mouth. "I like that very much," she said to B.J. "Granny sounds just fine."

"Then you'll sleep with me, Granny?"

"I will not," said his granny, and then, "Oh, good heavens, Tony, still this miserable little car? Couldn't she at least have left you the station wagon?"

"Mother, please. Look, things are going to be a bit crowded. Just let me get these bags stowed away, and then you kids pile in back—take your grandmother's bag there, Taylor, that shopping bag or whatever it is, and you'll sit in front, Mother—"

"I want to sit on Granny's lap!" shouted B.J. "I'm not gonna sit in back with them! I'm gonna—"

"You're going to sit where your father directs," said his grandmother.

"I will not!" B.J. banged his fist on the fender. "I'm not gonna sit with them and nobody can make me!"

"Very well. You may sit on my lap. But understand, that settles the matter of Go Fish or any reading. If you won't do what you're asked, you'll find you're not so easily obliged about what you ask. Do I make myself clear?"

B.J., mid-howl, grew silent and stood with his mouth open, considering the situation. "If I sit with them, you'll play Go Fish with me as soon as we get home?"

"No." When it became clear that he was about to

go on with his interrupted yell of fury, Grandmother Reddick said, "It's late, B.J. I've had a long trip. I'm tired. I expect you to understand simple things like that without being told. Long trip, tired, no Go Fish tonight. You understand?" He nodded skeptically. "Tomorrow, however, you and I shall continue with *Winnie-the-Pooh* where I left off last time, and we'll play as many games of Go Fish as I have time for. What do you say to that?"

B.J. climbed into the back seat. Exchanging a glance, Jem and Taylor got in beside him. Tony saw his mother into the front seat, went around and got behind the wheel. He took a deep breath, turned the ignition key and they started home.

5

"So—how's it going?" Sandy asked. "I called once, and got Jem."

"He told me."

"Why didn't you call back? It's been days."

"We've been housecleaning."

"Well, you expected that."

"I didn't know the lengths we'd go to."

"I guessed."

Taylor smiled and thought, How clean and shiny Sandy always looks. Like a seashell. Fingernails and toenails buffed pink. That faint smell of sandalwood. All of Sandy's—aura—was like that. This big room in which they sat was so wonderfully uncluttered. It had been done by a decorator, with stuff that the traveling Howards had picked up in different countries. An Italian bedstead, a Swiss wardrobe, Japanese tables low to the ground, lots of huge cushions covered with batik prints. There was one tremendous painting of huge yellow lemons against a black background. On a cushion of her own, tiny Viva slept with her paws crossed. Even the dog was dainty.

Taylor admired this room. She didn't envy it, because it wasn't her sort of place. At all. Here even the bookshelves, though completely filled, were in order. In her own room, nothing was in order. Of course, in her house there were no maids to keep things swept and polished. The maids, or couples, at the Howards' deserted on a regular basis, but were always quickly replaced because the quarters over the garage were so attractive. But I'd sure hate to work for them, Taylor thought. Mrs. Howard was usually pressing on toward her next hangover. Mr. Howard was arrogant and loud. Sandy said that where other people were concerned—family, employees or transient help—her father was absolutely without a clue. "It's as if he didn't know that other people actually have feelings, you know? The way some people can't believe that animals do."

"Taylor," Sandy said now, "you're thinking. I can tell. You've got an expression of cerebration. Of, I'll go so far as to say, ratiocination."

"That from a girl who spells tomato with an e."

"What matters is to know what words mean, and then to use them with spirit. How they're spelled is secondary. Funny about tomato, though. It looks as if it should have an e. What were you thinking about?"

"I thought you didn't like people to ask that."

"Now you're asking me to be *consistent*?"

"Well, I was wondering if I'd ever heard you say anything nice about your parents."

"That's a biggie. Lessee—there was that time about a year ago . . . But no, I ended by telling the truth, so that doesn't count. But there was that other time back in . . . No, no, that didn't come out to unqualified praise either. Give me a minute, I may come up with something."

"Didn't you ever care for them?"

"Well, of course it's entirely possible. I don't have a long personal memory. I can recall reams of poetry and prose, but where the id is concerned I seem to develop daily amnesia. Is develop spelled with three e's?"

"No."

"Tell me about your grandmother. Is it easier or harder, having her there? I mean, than you expected."

"I don't know. It's— Well, it's like, she never says a word against Junie. But everything she does, even the way she *touches* things, makes Junie out a slob."

"You've called her that yourself. Face it, you guys don't live in a sterile medium. You should look at it from her point of view. If you can."

"I try. I know all she gave up, and all she's enduring, and how hot it is, and how grateful we ought to be and we *are.* I mean, B.J.'s practically human, not like some terrible troll under the bridge. And I don't mind if the house is clean. I don't even mind having to clean it. But it's crazy, how she keeps uncovering embarrassing bits we didn't even know were there."

"Like what?"

"Like yesterday Jem got out some cheese straws he'd made. Ages ago, but anyway. He carried a bowl of them up to Grandmother Reddick. She was having iced tea in her room and we were keeping her company and Jem thought he'd give her a treat. And just when she started to eat one, she leaned over and looked in the dish and said what's that jumping around on the cheese straws—"

"Jumping on the cheese straws? What was, for Pete's sake?"

"Weevils."

"Weevils! How long had they been there?"

"That's what she wanted to know. We had to go look in the kitchen cupboards, and they were in *everything,* Sandy. The flour and the cornmeal and the crackers. Oh, boy. We had to clean all the cupboards and throw everything out and buy all new."

"All this time," Sandy said carefully, "all this time

when you haven't been noticing them, you've been *cooking* with weevils in the cornmeal and the flour and so forth?"

Taylor nodded.

"So you've been eating weevils."

"I guess so."

Sandy burst out laughing, and then said, "What am I laughing for? I've been eating them, too. When I think of the quiche and the cookies and *puff* pastry—"

"At least you can laugh. Grandmother Reddick isn't laughing. We offend her. Not just with weevils. The way we live, the way we think. Things we've just always taken for granted. The other evening Jem and B.J. and I were swimming in the bayou, naked, like always, and she came over looking for B.J., and when she saw us her face got red as a *beet,* and she said it was shameless and we ought to be ashamed of ourselves. She shouldn't make us feel ashamed, and I hate it."

"Did you feel ashamed?"

"With her carrying on like that? Wouldn't you?"

"Like Adam and Eve all of a sudden knowing they were undressed. My advice is, go along with your grandmother's whims. It'll keep the peace, and it won't be forever."

"Just till B.J.'s grown up," Taylor said bitterly.

"You really don't think Junie's coming back? You don't think she just has to get something out of her system and then she'll be back? I know if I were a woman and my husband gave me *household* money once a week, like a kid getting an allowance, I think at some point I'd go off and reflect on the situation. Doesn't mean I wouldn't come back."

"But Tony says that's the only way he can keep us from going into debt. Oh—I don't know, I don't know. I don't even know what I think she ought to do, anymore. I mean, when she first left, I just thought it was horrible and cruel. Walking out that way. Not even saying goodbye to B.J. But sometimes, Sandy, I think—maybe she had to? Do it that way? I mean, in a different way, Tony's as much of a male supremacy freak as your father. You know something? I think people are crazy to get married. A person must have enough trouble figuring out what to do just with her own life without adding on a lot of other people to worry about. Husbands, kids. I am *not* going to have any children." She sat with bowed shoulders, as if already weighted by the burden of her children's problems. And her parents', and her brothers'. Even Grandmother Reddick's. *She,* after all, hadn't asked to have her middle-aged Massachusetts coolth and comfort invaded by her son's troubles. By weevils in the cornmeal and children swimming naked in the bayou.

"There's this enormous color television set coming," she told Sandy. "Grandmother Reddick bought it."

"Why do you go on calling her Grandmother Reddick? You don't have another grandmother. It can't seem warm and welcoming to her. I realize that Granny's beyond your grasp, but just plain Grandmother should be possible."

"I call her that when I'm with her. B.J. calls her Granny."

"That's cute. I'm glad for her."

"The little black-and-white TV is going to go up in her room."

"You should hang on to that. It'll be an antique someday, probably, like old cars from the fifties."

"It'll be nice to see the animal programs in color, I guess." Taylor sighed, then lifted her voice plaintively and said what she'd been wanting to say for days but had been trying not to, out of loyalty. Grandmother Reddick, after all, was her family, and Sandy was not. But Sandy was her friend, and Grandmother was not. "She isn't the same person she used to be. She's somebody different!"

"Your grandmother?"

"Yes. My grandmother. Granny Reddick. She says and does things she'd never dare do if Junie were here."

"Like what?"

"Changing the furniture around. It doesn't sound like much, but she just *changes* things, without saying anything to us. She took down Junie's intaglio of fish skeletons. Jem found it in a closet and hung it in his room."

"The one of the two fish that killed each other?"

"Yes." It had been, despite its theme—two wide-mouthed fish that had met head-on so violently that one had choked and the other smothered—a beautiful print. As Junie said, the bones of fish were lovely to look at.

"So—that isn't very nice of her, but not actually unforgivable, Taylor."

"Oh, that's not all. It's how she makes us feel. Anyway, me. I wanted to *slink* home that evening we were swimming. I hate feeling like that. Or the way we eat. In the old days, when she visited, we ate mostly her way, out of politeness. Junie would say she was just visiting, and we could put up with stuffing in chickens, and pot roasts, and Waldorf salads and no onions or garlic in anything and *never* any fish or at least hardly ever and if we did she had to have something special because she hates fish. *And* eating at five-thirty because she's got in the habit of it, living alone. I don't see why you should eat at five-thirty because you live alone. And every day at breakfast she says what shall we plan for the evening meal. Evening meal . . . what an expression . . . and we never planned an *evening meal* at breakfast in our lives before and now we do it every day. And do you know, she has B.J. going to bed at seven-thirty! The first night he yelled and kicked up a fuss and she *spanked* him with her Daniel Green—"

"What's a Daniel Green?"

"Bedroom slipper. He was so astounded he stopped yelling and just went to bed, but then he got out again right away of course and do you know what she did then?"

"I feel sure you're going to tell me."

"She *put* this Daniel Green at the foot of his bed, after he was back in it, and she said next time he was tempted to get up and go charging around when it was past his bedtime, he was just to look at that slipper, lying there . . . *ready.*"

"I think that's neat."

"Neat! Sandy, that is practically corporal punishment—"

"Oh, come off it, Taylor. Look, you were losing your acorns over B.J., you and Jem. He had the two of you in some sort of Saint Vitus's dance, trying to keep him in line, even trying to keep him alive, come to that. And your grandmother brings him into line just with a bedroom slipper. Only one? Not a pair?"

"One," Taylor said sullenly.

"Absolutely whizzo. Unless, of course, she beats him unmercifully with this Daniel Green. Does she bang away at his little tush till it bleeds?"

"Don't be dumb."

"You're jealous because you didn't think of it yourself. Of course, you're at a disadvantage, not being the owner of a Daniel Green."

"We never hit anyone in our family."

"Probably just what B.J. needed. Maybe, come to think of it, just what he wanted. I read somewhere that children who are never disciplined are actually miserable. It's because they feel no one really cares enough to discipline them, so they make these little rushes into mischief, all designed to make their parents haul them back into line. They're longing to be aligned, so to speak. And when no one pays attention to their first forays off the path of righteousness, they're away and running. Drugs, shoplifting, truancy, kinky sex—" She broke off, turning her head to one side, like an animal considering a strange noise. "Did you ever think, Taylor, what an awful *nuisance* all that must be?"

"I never thought about it at all."

Sandy seemed, for a moment, at a loss for words. Then she said, "You are truly amazing. I mean you're so straight arrow you don't even know there's a choice, do you?"

"You don't have to condescend to me, Sandy. I know that stuff goes on. I know there's a—counterculture. I didn't say I didn't know about it, I said I didn't think about it."

"Don't be cross."

"I'm not cross. I was just trying to point out—"

She never finished the sentence. A shriek of penetrating shrillness chopped it in midair.

Scrambling to their feet, Sandy and Taylor ran to the hall landing where Amanda, arms folded above her head, body twisting from side to side, let out scream after scream. As they watched, she ran stumbling down the stairs.

"You can't, you can't, you can't! You cannot go and leave me in this world alone! You *promised* me . . ."

Backed against a table in the foyer was a weedy frail youth in gray slacks and a powder-blue cotton-knit pullover. His eyes were wild and frightened.

"Hey!" Sandy yelled. "Hey, Amanda! What's going

on? Why are you making that awful noise?"

Amanda flung herself at the young man, who staggered, trying either to fend her off or hold her up, and the two of them fell to the floor. Amanda swarmed over him like a lizard, beating her fists on his shoulders.

Sandy ran down the stairs, Taylor following, and tried to pull her sister away. "What *are* you doing, Amanda? Have you gone clear around the bend? You cut it out, or so help me I'll call the cops!"

Amanda stopped her pummeling, sat up, dropped on her arms, crying noisily. "He promised me, he promised me," she sobbed, clenching and unclenching her fists. "I'm going to die—"

The boy got shaking to his feet, stood wiping spittle from his mouth. "Geez," he said. "What the hell."

Sandy stared at him. "My god, it's Alexander, isn't it?"

He nodded, his wary gaze on Amanda on the floor. If I'd passed him on the street, thought Taylor, I never would have guessed. Hair cut almost short, beard gone, beads gone, clean clothes, no smell. Alexander had been the smelliest human being on the island. Now he stood before them, glossy and fragrant, looking a dewy fourteen.

"Are you in disguise, or coming out of it?" Sandy asked.

"I'm leaving for the north, for Princeton. I'm going to visit some friends on the way. I just came to say goodbye to Amanda, that's all. I never promised her a meaningful relationship, or anyway not a lasting meaningful relationship—"

"Are you old enough to go to college?" Taylor asked.

"He did too promise! You *promised* me, Alexander—"

"I never did," Alexander said to Sandy. "I thought we were just having a good time, and I thought I oughta come around and say good-bye and look what happens. I mean, hell—"

Amanda leaned dramatically back on her hands and stared up at him through half-shut lids. "You violated me," she said. "And I'm going to tell my father on you."

"Hey, that's not so! You *know* it isn't, Amanda." He turned to Sandy. "We never even made it, not really. And she knows it." Sandy shrugged, and Alexander turned to look down at Amanda on the floor. "Why're you doing this? You're spoiling everything, you know. I mean, we had a dynamite time, and maybe when I come down at Christmas, or even Thanksgiving—"

Amanda, who despite terrible posture moved with grace, now wafted to her feet. "Dynamite times!" she said in a voice of scorn, and Alexander backed against the table again, putting his hands on it behind him for support. Taylor rather admired him for standing his ground. He could easily have just run out the door and away. Imagine admiring Alexander.

"You poor creepy-crawly," Amanda said. "There's more dynamite in a kitchen match than there is in you. And you made a terrible mistake, let me tell you, when you shaved that beard and showed your puny naked little chin to the world." She flicked him on the newly bared chin with her finger, hard enough to make him wince. "You have never—not ever—laid a hand on me, you understand? I've never been so much as breathed on by you, and if you tell my father anything different, he'll thrash you on the village green. Be off! I'll have the dogs on you!"

Viva, on cue, appeared on the landing above, barking as Amanda went up the stairs, one hand against the wall, stumbling slightly.

"Be *off*?" Sandy said, looking after her sister with a worried frown. "What do you suppose she's been reading?"

"I wonder what she's been smoking," said Taylor.

Sandy rounded on Alexander, who was making for the door. "Hey! Hey, you! Did you give her grass? I want to *know*. Have you been giving her *any* kind of stuff?"

Alexander said coldly, "No, I have not. I haven't given her a thing. And I do mean, not a damn thing. I'd check your mother's liquor supply, if I were you."

"Why you—you—"

"Try creepy-crawly," Alexander suggested, and at that moment Mr. Howard entered in a fever of ill humor, trailed by Jem and Dan, looking exceedingly nervous. Alexander, sensing that this anger was not directed against him, started again for the door but was stopped by J. Ellis Howard, who barked, "Who in hell are you?"

"Alexander, sir. I just shaved my beard is all."

Sir, thought Taylor, without surprise. Bathed, debeaded and debearded, Alexander emerged a natural sir sayer.

"Did a lot besides shave your beard. It's the first time I haven't had to hold my nose when you were in the room."

"What I like about this family," said Sandy, "is its firm grasp of the concept of courtesy."

"Hold your tongue," said her father and continued down the hall to his den, where he snatched up the telephone, dialed a number he clearly had by heart and snapped, "J. Ellis Howard here. Give me the Chief."

"Sandy, I think we'll go, okay?" said Taylor. Alexander had already made his escape. "C'mon, Jem."

" 'Bye," said Sandy. She was still looking anxiously up the stairs. Amanda had disappeared. She turned to Dan, who was scratching his head and shifting from one foot to another while their father shouted into the telephone, demanding to speak to the Chief of Police.

"What's this all about?" Sandy asked her brother, as Taylor and Jem went out.

"What *is* it all about?" Taylor asked as they pedaled through the peaceful village, taking their time.

"Oh, boy," said Jem. "We think we got troubles with Grandmother. I think Dan's got more troubles than fifty other guys rolled together. . . ."

6

Jem and Dan had been to a movie in town. Afterward, they'd gone for a cone at Baskin-Robbins, then walked around to Mr. Howard's central bank. He'd said he'd drive them back up to the island when the movie was over. They'd taken the bus in and would have preferred to take it back, but Dan had persuaded Jem not to turn down the offer from his father. It made Dan nervous to turn down offers from his father. It made both boys nervous to drive with him, but Jem conceded that they did not have much choice.

They sat in the back seat, telling each other what a rotten movie it had been, but in a little while grew silent and concentrated on the driver. Jem, who preferred any boat, no matter what kind or size, to any car, even one as fancy as this, thought that it was funny how men always seemed to think they were good drivers. Mr. Howard, who had to be the world's shaggiest, surely couldn't know it. He, like Tony, always took the wheel. Tony wouldn't let Junie drive even her own station wagon if he was in it, though in Jem's opinion his mother was a better driver.

"When are you gonna get more fish?" Dan said loudly, wrenching his gaze away from the front seat. "You haven't got any fish in ages."

Jem had two salt-water aquariums that he had built by himself. Well, with a little help from Dan. He kept them stocked with small fish he snorkeled for in the bay. About every three weeks he emptied both aquariums and started over again. He said it was so the fish would not be imprisoned too long, but Dan thought it was for the fun of emptying, refilling, rearranging rocks and weeds and then going into the bay to net a fresh supply of hostages. Dan was a tremendous admirer of Jem's aquariums. He was a tremendous admirer of Jem, who was all Dan thought a guy should be—skinny, tough, tireless, kind. He'd never known Jem to say a mean thing about anybody. He supposed Jem didn't even think mean things. Not like me, Dan thought. I think mostly mean things, I guess.

His attention was dragged back to his father's voice. Mr. Howard had got behind one of those slow-moving cars that are part of the Florida scene, and was carrying on a low conversation with himself. ". . . damn stupid fools—ought to have their licenses yanked. What can the police be thinking of? . . . like to know the damn fool quack that signed this imbecile up for another term of legal menace by machine—paid off, *I'll* bet—"

The road up the island was a two-laner, with occasional places for turning and passing. Jem and Dan had observed several spots at which Mr. Howard could have gone around the crawling car, but apparently he had not noticed, or had been too angry to. Now, as the double yellow line appeared, together with an automobile in the oncoming lane, Mr. Howard swerved widely, turned to gesticulate at the driver beside him, pulled back to his own lane as the car opposite swerved, its horn blaring, into a motel parking lot.

"Jeez," said Dan, slumping nearly to his neck.

Jem glanced at the driver in the slow car. An old lady whose eyes seemed to be on a level with the steering wheel. No wonder she had to drive so slow. Couldn't see where she was going, probably.

Jem, breathing hard, exchanged a glance with Dan. Then, at a sound behind them, they turned and saw a motorcycle policeman coming up fast behind them. He had to go fast because Mr. Howard was speeding. To get away from the other angry driver. To put the old turtle of a lady far behind him. For some reason. Anyway, speeding. And here came the cops.

"Dad," said Dan, leaning forward. "Hey, there's a cop right behind you. He's telling us to stop."

"Nonsense," said Mr. Howard, as the motorcycle glided beside him and the policeman made a firm, unmistakable gesture.

Mr. Howard muttered, pulled to the side and looked out the window as the law got off its bike, adjusted the stand, walked in no hurry toward the car, pulling a book from its hip pocket, a pen from its shirt pocket.

"Now, see here, Officer," Mr. Howard began. "Oh, it's you, Carl. Well, I want to explain—"

"Mr. Howard," said the policeman, "you went over a double line, with a car in the other lane practically on your hood. If that guy hadn't pulled into the Hilton parking lot there'd have been a— It would've been awful. Awful. And I clocked you going seventy away from the scene—"

"Scene? What are you talking about, man? There was no accident, so there was no *scene.*"

"There would've been, if it had been up to you. I had to stop and reassure the old lady, and then talk the driver of the other car out of coming back to knock your block off, which is how I happened to catch you going seventy by the time I caught up—"

"Do you know that one of these radar scanners clocked a *tree* going at seventy miles an hour? And now you're trying to tell me—"

The young policeman held up his hand. "It wasn't radar doing the clocking. It was me, on my bike. And I clocked you at seventy, same as the tree, so—"

"Carl, I don't care for your tone. Not one bit."

The policeman's face reddened. "License and registration, please," he said.

"Now look here—"

"If you please." The policeman held out his hand. He glanced at the boys in the back seat. Jem detected sympathy in his eyes. I'm never going to ride with this guy again, he thought. Never. For any reason. Dan's stuck and can't do anything about it, but I'm not and I can and I'm going to. He looked at his friend, but Dan had his eyes closed and he didn't open them again until his father had pulled up outside the big garage. "You two come with me," he said, marching toward the front door. "I may need you as witnesses."

"Witnesses?" Dan croaked. "Ah, gee—"

"Look, Dan," Jem whispered. "I'm just gonna split, okay?"

"Jem!"

A cry from the depths of Dan's tubby frame. Jem could do nothing but follow him into the house, where they encountered a weird scene with a dude who turned out to be Alexander without a beard looking like he'd just lost a round with Dracula, and Sandy looking, for the first time Jem could remember, jumpy as a cat, and Viva barking and dancing around, sliding on marble floors, and Taylor blinking nervously all around.

“So that’s what’s happened,” Jem said to his sister, typically not asking about the scene in the Howard hallway. “I mean, Taylor—Grandmother’s a pain in the neck in some ways, how picky she is and everything, but she doesn’t scare the pants off you, the way that guy does. And she’d never try to bribe a cop, either.”

“He doesn’t scare Sandy,” Taylor said.

“Oh, she’s scareproof. Of course, I’ve never seen her when she was in a car her old man was driving. That’d be the test.”

Sandy had been frightened watching her sister this afternoon. Clear out of her tree, Amanda had been. And all for the love of *Alexander*? It didn’t seem possible. Could hurt pride make a person behave like that? Or was Sandy right, and Amanda was actually a bit bananas? If so, how horrible for her, and for her family.

“I remember,” she said to her brother, “that Junie once said it’s a wonder the human condition doesn’t make cowards of us all.”

He glanced over at her. It was the first time since their mother had left that Taylor had mentioned her this way. Not angrily, not bitterly, just repeating something she’d said because it seemed to fit. Like quoting a book you’d once read, a person you’d once known. Does that mean I’m forgiving her, or forgetting her? Taylor wondered. She didn’t know. She had no way of getting in touch with her feelings about Junie, and generally tried to hold them off altogether. Like Scarlett in the movie, she’d rather think about it tomorrow.

7

Tut and Drum were sitting together at the back door and rose hopefully as Taylor and Jem came down the driveway.

"Look at that," Taylor said. "She's put them out again. Every time we go out, she does that. You'd think it wasn't their house at all. Just because they shed a little, for Pete's sake. Jem, you could at least answer me!"

"You didn't ask anything. What's to answer, anyway? They probably don't care. Anybody with sense would rather be outdoors than indoors." He let the animals into a house redolent of cooking. "Meat loaf?" he said, sniffing. "Pot roast?"

"Stew, I bet," said Taylor, thinking of the days of cold soup, seviche, broiled fish, shrimp salad, hazelnut mousse. Now, no matter how hot it was, they had meat loaf, potatoes, cakes or pies. Stew. Cooked by Grandmother Reddick. Taylor and Jem had just about stopped cooking, since they couldn't learn to do it her way. Grandmother Reddick used ReaLemon instead of real lemons, because it was easier. She used all kinds of instant and frozen things that had never been in the house before. Frozen pie crusts. Instant topping, nondairy. And Tony never said a word.

In the living room, Taylor looked around suspiciously. It seemed that not only were the animals exiled the minute she and Jem turned their backs, but every time they returned something had happened to make their house cleaner, tidier, less homey. The rugs had been sent out and returned too clean for animals to lie on. The mother-of-pearl design on the coffee table showed nicely now, since all that was displayed on it was a copy of the *National Geographic* and a soapstone seal carved by Eskimos and bought by Junie at a flea market. All the woodwork had been scrubbed, all the windows washed, and Grandmother Reddick was engaged in making, in her room with the air-conditioner and Junie's sewing machine, a set of slipcovers to replace the tacky loose covers that Junie had made long ago.

"Jem!" she said. "Where are Junie's shells?"

Their mother's shells (which she said was not a collection but an accumulation) had been gathered over the years and distributed around the house in rows on windowsills, in piles on bookcase shelves, in heaps and arrangements upstairs and down. For months there'd been a lot of them, in a bowl Taylor liked, in the center of the dining-room table. Now the shells were gone, and the bowl too.

"Well," Taylor muttered. "Well. There isn't a thing safe here anymore at all. That's what it comes to."

Jem, who was trying to keep the peace by not taking or listening to anybody's side, looked upset. "What's happened to them, do you think?"

"I'll find out, don't you worry."

"Taylor, please. Don't get anything started, huh? Tony'll come in and find out."

"Find out what? Have *I* started anything? Have I said one word about the way she goes in our rooms to see if we've made the beds and cleaned up *properly* and taken our clothes down to the laundry room? Have I *mentioned* that she feels free to straighten up the things on my desk, and she's *told* me I don't need so much material on birds, a lot of it's just dust collecting? Have I said a word about all the snoopiness and criticism and spying, have I?"

"Cut it out! She doesn't *spy*. Who'd want to spy on you? Taylor, please just let it go, huh? I can't stand any more fighting in this house. I really can't."

"Peace at any price, that's your motto?"

"Maybe. She's an old lady—"

"You better not let her hear you saying that. She's a middle-aged secret agent, that's what she is."

"Oh, knock it off," Jem snapped. "You give me a pain. She's doing the best she can. She didn't *ask* to come here. Just because her ways are different from ours—"

"I wonder what she'd say if we went up to Lexington and messed her house all up? Suppose we sat all the puff out of her down cushions and made the pictures hang crooked and tramped mud in from outside. Would she say we were doing the best we could and our ways were different from hers? I'll tell you something, Jem . . . she has no respect for children. Not that I consider myself a child, but she does. And she has no real respect for me or you or even her darling B.J. You don't see her prowling around Tony's room putting things in order, do you?"

"Shut up, will you? I'm tired of listening to you!" Taylor's eyes brimmed, and Jem said hastily, "I take it back, I take it back! Jeez, aren't we ever going to have any peace around here? I'm going to take the canoe over to Wrasse Island. Where's Drum? I'm gonna take him with me. He and Tut are the only decent company there is around here anymore."

"You can't take the canoe now. There's a storm coming."

While they'd been talking, the storm that threatened

every afternoon at about this time of day at this time of year had piled itself together in the sky. Herds of elephant-gray clouds moved massively over the Gulf, over the bay. Lightning fell in flashing veins from sky to sea, filled the atmosphere with a shaking pallor, quivered into darkness again. Thunder cracked and roared overhead, then boomed in the distance.

They walked out on the dock and stood facing the wind, breathing deeply. "I don't think it's going to rain," said Jem. "It's just gonna holler around and then go away." But he was too smart to go out on the water while lightning menaced the air, so they just watched while pelicans and terns and cormorants beat their way against the wind to safe roosting places, listened to the slap and suck of waves around the pilings. A convoy of porpoises—undisturbed by weather, wind or restless waters—came through the pass from Gulf to bay, their glistening long bodies serenely arching as they lifted from the waves long enough to breathe before sliding back in again.

"I'm going in and find out about those shells," Taylor said. "Are you coming?"

"No way."

"Suit yourself."

She walked down the dock, turned at the door to look back. Jem had got into a rope hammock Tony had slung between two pilings at the end of the dock. A person could just about disappear in that hammock. Jem was shutting out the world and wouldn't leave his cocoon unless the rains drove him from it. She glanced at the sky, still roiling with clouds, rumbling and tossing bright bolts but withholding the deluge. The tops of the Australian pines swayed and sighed in a wind that sent palm fronds streaming and set bamboo canes creaking against one another. It was often like this, like the setting of a tremendous stage set, with no act to follow.

At her grandmother's door she hesitated. The television was on, of course. It was just about always on now, and B.J. was just about always perched in front of it, goggling goofily, as if he'd forgotten that the world was outside. He never went out anymore with her or Jem in the canoe or the Sunfish. He turned down Tony's occasional offer of a sail on *Loon*. He didn't fish off the dock, or beg Taylor to take him to the beach when she went over there. He clung to his grandmother, and since she almost never left the house because of the heat and the mosquitoes, and since she nearly always had the TV running, though often she was not looking at it, it followed that B.J. watched the thing for hours every day. And B.J. gave it his all. Short of turning it off or hitting him on the head, you couldn't get his attention when it was once fixed on that world in a box.

It'll get worse, Taylor thought, when the new one she's bought arrives. Huge. In color. They'd be lucky if he didn't forget how to talk.

"Damn," she muttered, and knocked on her grandmother's door.

The window air-conditioner was on high. It was noisy, and the room quite cold. B.J., watching a hospital drama, didn't turn, but Grandmother Reddick, at the sewing machine, looked up and smiled. "There you are, dear. Where have you been?"

"At Sandy's."

"Such an interesting girl. But she does think a lot of herself, doesn't she?"

"That's what makes her so good to know."

"I don't think I quite understand?"

"Well, along with Amy March and the entire Dobkin clan, Sandy has the most gorgeous self-image of anyone I've ever read about or met. And it makes her good to know, that's all."

"She's certainly a *neat* child, but surely a bit stout to have such a fine—self-image, as you call it? In my day, fat girls weren't generally so pleased with themselves."

Taylor stiffened, but did not respond. Whether Jem believed it or not, she did a lot of refraining around Tony's mother, who was not, despite the big sacrifice, a very nice person. In the past, when Grandmother Reddick had come visiting, Junie had always been immaculately polite to her, and that was what Taylor was trying to be now. She hadn't realized, until now, that being polite involved more than watching your manners. It required a knack for hypocrisy.

"Grandmother," she said, in what certainly felt like an amiable tone, "what's happened to Junie's shells? I was just wondering, you know . . ."

"Nothing's *happened* to them, Taylor. You surely didn't think I'd throw them away, did you?"

"I certainly did not." Such a terrible thought hadn't entered her mind. "Junie's been collecting them for years. It's a beautiful—accumulation. I just was wondering what hap— where they are."

"In a box in the garage. I cannot have the house cluttered with dust collectors. The shells will be safe enough stored in the garage. So strange to live in a country where there are no cellars for storage purposes."

Another *country*? Taylor thought. That's how she sees it? Jem was right. She was making a huge, a really unacceptable sacrifice, coming down here. In another year—*year*!—B.J. could go to kindergarten, and then Grandmother Reddick could go back to her country, to Massachusetts, to her cellar and her bridge games and her goose-down cushions. Anybody could get through a year. How?

"Where's the bowl that we had full of shells on the dining-room table? Junie bought that bowl at a sale and she's awfully fond of it."

"I should think so. It's a Lowestoft tureen and extremely valuable. Criminal to have it just sitting around where it might easily get broken. I've looked for a piece of Lowestoft for years and never been able to find one and your mother just picks it up and doesn't even know what it is. I have it safely packed away."

"How do you know she doesn't know what it is?"

"She wouldn't just leave it lying around where it could

get broken—children and animals running around all day. An object like that must be taken *care* of. My goodness, if your mother had always had the shrewdness to pick a thing like that. But I've looked around, and there isn't anything else of real value. Some pretty things, but not in a class with that tureen. There now, you do understand, don't you?"

"Yes."

"Yes—what?" Grandmother Reddick said gently.

"Yes, Grandmother."

At five-thirty, eating stew, she thought, what's the difference? Who cares? Junie gone, the shells gone, Tony practically never home. He was still working extra hours because of the pastry chef's bad back. He said. Jem and Taylor thought he was making it up in order to stay away as much as possible. B.J. a zombie, Jem about as approachable as a horse conch in its shell. But what difference did it make that their lives were altered past recall? People's lives were altered past recall all the time, in ways far worse than anything that was happening to them in this house.

After dinner, Jem and Taylor loaded the dishwasher. Then Taylor got her binoculars and informed her grandmother that she was going over to walk on the beach. "Want to come along, B.J.?" she asked. "Come on, honey. There are hundreds of marvelous birds. I saw a black-necked stilt the other day. There's a breeze, so we could take a kite. How about it?"

Before B.J. had a chance to turn her down, Grandmother Reddick said, "Taylor, I prefer that you not go over to that beach by yourself at this hour. There's no knowing who might be there. Hippies. I must ask you not to go."

Was there any point in telling her that all the hippies were gone with the wind? No, no point.

She said, "Grandmother, I've been going to the beach to walk and fly kites and look at birds and swim and—and be *alive*—all my life, and I'm not going to stop going there now."

Looking at Jem and B.J., Grandmother Reddick lowered her voice. "You are not a child any longer, Taylor. You are a young lady. Young girls are prey to all sorts of—dangers."

"You mean someone's going to drag me into the bushes and rape me?" Taylor said loudly. She was not sorry to see her grandmother's face flush. Whispering in front of the boys about *female* things. It was awful.

"I think it's disgraceful—disgusting—the way you children talk," Grandmother Reddick said in a shaken tone. "If this is how June's brought you up, it may be just as well—"

"Tony's been around, Grandmother. Don't forget about him. He's been around, too, bringing us up, hearing how we talk."

They faced each other, the girl and the middle-aged woman, closer to declared discord than they'd allowed themselves to get before. Taylor's mouth was dry, her pulse quick, and she thought she saw in her grandmother's expression a trace of alarm. Irony, she decided, as the silence between them grew into something threatening. I only told her I was going to the beach in order to be polite. If I'd kept still and just gone, we'd have avoided this. And had it to face another time.

"You heard me, Taylor," said Grandmother Reddick. She put her fingers to her forehead and massaged it, as if soothing an ache. It was a gesture Tony had when he was upset, or worried, or sad. "I expect," she went on, "to be obeyed. As long as I've been put in this situation, I expect obedience from you children."

"Okay," said Taylor. She walked out on the dock, leaving the door open behind her. I hope mosquitoes get in, she thought. Clouds and clouds of mosquitoes. I hope cockroaches fly into her air-conditioner and get ground up and spatter all over her when she's asleep. I hope—

"Taylor?"

"Hi, Jem," she said listlessly. "Nice kettle of fish we're in. Or should I say kettle of Irish stew."

"I'm sorry about it."

"Not your fault, Jem."

"No, but I should've stuck up for you. I should've said something when she said that about Junie. I think— You know something, Taylor, I think I'm a coward. I can't stand upsets. *Confrontations.* They make me sick to my stomach."

"Probably that stew."

"I'm serious, Taylor. I think I'm the kind of person who betrays his friends and his country when he's subjected to torture or temptation."

"For Pete's sake, Jem—you've been watching that damned television set again. You aren't a coward, you aren't old enough to be a coward, and you're not going to grow up to be a coward, you hear?"

"How do you know?"

"I know. Just take my word for it, okay?"

"Okay."

"It's been a horrible day, just horrible. But there's nothing we can do about it, so what's the use of talking. Jem—she said I couldn't go to the beach alone. She didn't say anything about two of us. I can't because I'm a young lady, but two of us are just a couple of kids, right?"

"I guess—" he began.

"It's settled. We'll go over and swim and walk and not talk or think or do anything but look at the birds and watch the sunset."

"Won't set till eight o'clock. Six after, to be exact."

"So, we'll wait. Sunset over the Gulf is worth waiting for."

The west coast of Florida is the only place on the east coast of the United States where you can see the sun sink into the ocean. That was not a miracle that Taylor meant to be deprived of, for any reason, by anybody.

"Well," she said, "are you coming?"

Jem hesitated, then agreed. Taylor knew he was reluctant, afraid of stirring up Grandmother Reddick's already fretful feelings. But she knew, too, that once at the beach, floating on the wide waves, watching flocks of birds cross the sky as they made for inland nests and roosting places, watching the sun transfigure sky and sea, he'd forget the day just past, stop flinching from days to come. He would, and so would she. For a while.

8

The pastry chef returned to work and offered to take over for Tony for a couple of days, so on Thursday morning Tony came out on the dock early and sat in one of the old canvas chairs with his coffee, staring at the bright penny water of the bay. After a while he observed a form in the hammock and got up to investigate. There was his daughter, curled on her side, asleep. As he stood looking down at her, she stirred, turned, blinked at him and smiled.

"What're you doing out here?" she asked, yawning.

"I could inquire that of you."

"I sleep out here lots of times. I mean," she said, swinging around and getting to her feet, "I have insomnia, I guess. Sometimes if I come down here and lie and look at the stars, I fall asleep finally." She stretched. "I'll get some orange juice. If I try to go upstairs I might wake Grandmother up, so I can't brush my teeth for now."

She looked at her father closely, to see what sort of mood he was in. This morning he seemed pretty good. Not in such a *moody* mood as usual. His eyes were heavy and red rimmed, but that was probably because he didn't get enough sleep. Who was sleeping well in this house? Even B.J. still yelled out in his dreams, Jem said.

"How about some eggs benedict?" Tony asked.

"Oh, that'd be super. Look, suppose I tiptoe in and get the boys and we'll all have breakfast together?"

"Don't do that, Taylor. Let's the two of us have breakfast together and talk."

Taylor looked at her feet, wondering about the quality of joy. It could come so suddenly, so unexpectedly, and leave you flat in a second. "I'm not really hungry," she said.

"You mean you don't want to talk to me."

"I mean—I suppose I mean that I don't want to be talked *at*. It sounds like some kind of lecture coming."

"Ah, Taylor—don't. Come into the kitchen and have some café au lait and sit with me while I fix us something good and I promise I won't talk at you. Just with you.

If you like. We can cook in Trappist silence if you prefer." Taylor smiled. "That's better. Like the old days."

Tony prepared a mug of café au lait, told her to perch on the kitchen stool and watch how a master did things. "Fix us a couple of mangoes when you're ready, will you, honey?" he asked, and Taylor got two of the large luscious fruits from a basket and prepared them as she'd been taught, scoring them still in the peel, then turning the halves back. A beautiful fruit, glistening like orange topazes.

"I guess you never know, when you're *in* the old days, how wonderful they are, do you?" she asked.

Tony, attending to his hollandaise, said without turning that he supposed that was true, for most people.

Maybe, she thought, these are olden days that we'll look back on sometime and think how wonderful they were. She didn't see how, but supposed it was possible. Something more horrible even than Junie's leaving could happen, and then she'd remember this morning, sitting with Tony, watching him crack eggs with one hand (something she and Jem couldn't do yet), slip them into simmering water while he slid English muffins into the toaster and laid strips of ham in the skillet all in what seemed a single flowing motion.

"I wonder how, out of all the things you could've been, you became a chef?" she asked. "There's nothing in your background that would *indicate* it. Or did your father enjoy food?"

"He enjoyed it—but the same way as my mother. Only

things he'd eaten all his life. You couldn't have got him to try a snail, or an oyster, say, any more than you could my mother."

"But they lived so close to Boston, and that's a famous seafood place."

"Not around my house. The day *I* tried a snail, in a French restaurant in Gloucester with a very pretty girl to lead me on, my whole life altered."

Taylor wondered about that pretty girl. Someone who'd perhaps been important in her father's life long before she was born. Before he'd even met Junie.

"Grandmother says mangoes are revolting. She says they smell unwholesome." She spoke and was immediately sorry. Her father's brisk motions slowed, his look of quiet pleasure drained away. He so rarely looked pleased and happy anymore, and now she'd gone and spoiled it.

"Are you so totally miserable with my mother?" he asked. "No, no—I'm not going to lecture you. I'm asking because I need to know. If you simply cannot tolerate her here, I'll try to work something else out. Try to explain to her . . ." He stopped.

"How?" Taylor asked.

Fingers rubbing his forehead, he was silent awhile before admitting he wasn't sure how. "But I am not going to sacrifice you children. I just won't have that."

"We're not being sacrificed. B.J.'s happy as a clam. And Jem—"

"What about Jem?"

"I think he just isn't facing things. So he's okay."

"What do you mean?"

"I think he thinks Junie's coming back. So he's waiting for that, and being pretty good meanwhile. I mean, when you consider that he had to empty his aquariums and not fill them again—"

"Why?" Tony said sharply.

"He slops water all over the place when he changes the fish. You know, Tony. He lets what he has in the tanks go back in the bay, and then he has to empty the old water and put in fresh, and then when he gets more fish to replace the old ones he carries them through the house in a bucket, and the water slops all over the floor and the boards have been polished and the rugs cleaned so Grandmother doesn't want them slopped on and when she found out he does this every three or four weeks and it's such a mess, she asked him to stop. Jem says it's okay. He says she's making all these nice new slipcovers and got the rugs cleaned and all, so he says he'll wait till next spring before he catches any new fish. So the aquariums just sit there, empty. And Junie's shells are all put away, and B.J.'s turning into an enormous eye like a Cyclops, and Tut and Drum can hardly ever get in the house anymore—"

"Here," said Tony. "These things are ready. I'll carry the tray. You bring the coffee pot. Hold the door open for me, Taylor."

When they were seated at the round table on the dock where they had so often eaten in the past but did not anymore, Tony said, "So you want me to ask her to leave?"

"No. I just want you to know how things are around here. You stay away all the time. We think you stay away more than you have to, because you don't like the way things are here. The atmosphere. And when you are here you're asleep or out in the boat or just absent in your head."

She and Jem had found they'd speak to their father and their words would hang for a while in the fog of his inattention and then presently he'd look up and glance around as though attracted by skywriting. "Did one of you say something?" he'd ask.

"You don't hear us," she told him now. "I think everything would be better if you'd just listen to us. And maybe stay home more. These are marvelous, Tony. You make the best hollandaise in the world."

"If I said I'd do that—listen to you, stay home when I can and be with you as much as possible—do you think you could resign yourself to my mother's presence?"

"You make me sound awful, you know. Saying things like tolerate, and resign myself. Just awful. Maybe I am awful. Grandmother and I seem to have some kind of personality clash. But Jem's right and I'm wrong. He says she's made a terrible sacrifice to come down here and be in the heat and put up with us and the mess and the bugs. Put up with me," she added. "I'm not really very polite to her."

"I'm sorry to hear that."

"She isn't polite to me, Tony! She *isn't.*"

"I'm sorry to hear that, too."

"I expect that's why you don't listen to us. Because you're sure that everything you hear is going to make you sorry."

"Maybe. I asked you, Taylor, if you thought you could adjust to having my mother here if I made a greater effort to—do my part."

"Sure, I could, Tony. Anyway—I've been thinking. In a year, B.J. can go to kindergarten, and then Grandmother could go back home, couldn't she? I mean, she really doesn't like being here at all—she's just doing it for you. And for B.J., of course. But don't you think she'd be awfully relieved to go back? I mean, if I had to live in Lexington and thought I'd never get back down here, I'd just plain die. So she must feel the same, only the other way around."

She wondered about Junie, living in Connecticut, going to work every day in New York City, which sounded like a horrible place. How could she stand it? Didn't she long for their house and the live oaks with air plants growing along their shaggy boughs and the wild orchids, and bamboo canes creaking in the wind, and the surf and the call of the night heron in the dark? Even if she doesn't miss us, Taylor thought, doesn't she miss mockingbirds? How can she stand not being *here*?

When she'd said that Jem expected Junie to come back to them, her father's expression hadn't changed, except maybe to become more expressionless. Tony didn't show his feelings easily. He was a man people liked but didn't get to know. That time he'd been sick and had to go to the hospital—all the people from the kitchen, and the waiters, and Jean-Jacques, who owned the restaurant, had come to see him. Even some of the clientele who knew him had sent flowers. But Tony didn't have real friends. He said when he wasn't working he wanted to be at home, and not bothered by people. So what it comes to, Taylor thought, is that he really only has us. And if we make things hard for him with Grandmother Reddick, he won't have peace or comfort anywhere. Exalted, she decided to love her grandmother for her father's sake.

A group of oyster catchers appeared from nowhere and landed on a sandbar that appeared in the bay at low tide. She watched them with joy. Seven of them. Seven wonderful oyster catchers. And now came a couple of black-bellied plovers, still in courting plumage. And a piping plover! The plover, she decided, was an omen of good days to come.

They'd been quiet for a long time, he in his self-communings and she in hers, but now she said, "Everything's going to be fine, Tony. You just wait and see."

The opportunity to act upon her resolution arrived as soon as Grandmother, trailed by B.J., came downstairs to breakfast. Not wanting to come out on the dock in the heat, she sent B.J. to inquire whether Tony wouldn't like to come in and have his second cup of coffee with her. Taylor, stacking her father's dishes and hers on the tray, said, "Go on, Tony. It's okay. But it was a lovely breakfast. And fun."

"Couldn't you come, too?" he asked.

Taylor hesitated, then nodded. "Sure. I'd love to."

"There's a nice breeze. Suppose we take *Loon* out after a while. Would you like that?"

"I'd love it."

Grandmother and B.J. had prunes, eggs, bacon and toast at the dining-room table, Tony and Taylor sitting with them for company.

"Where is Jem?" Grandmother asked.

"Still asleep," said B.J. "Got the pillow over his head and that sign he got from Howard Johnson's saying don't disturb him."

"Well," said Grandmother, "I think it would be best if we did disturb him. It's getting late, and we don't want people getting breakfasts all morning. B.J., run along in—"

"Mother," Tony interrupted, "it really doesn't matter if he sleeps. Let's just let him."

"But he's been sleeping this way every morning, Tony. I can't think it's good for him, and it does keep the kitchen in a mess. Besides, he'll be having to get up early for school soon, and if he's got in the habit of sleeping—"

"It'll be all right," Tony said gently. "Sit down, B.J."

"Well, I'm sure you know best," said Grandmother

Reddick, sounding quite that he did not. "But we'll let it pass. But there is one thing I have to speak to you about, Tony, very seriously. And I'm glad Taylor is here to hear it. . . ."

Taylor's elevated mood dimmed. What now? What had she done, or left undone, or looked as if she might be thinking of doing?

"I must talk to you about Taylor," Grandmother said to her son, then turned to her granddaughter, adding, "I wouldn't go behind your back about this, Taylor, but I've warned you about your habit of going over to the beach by yourself, and yesterday you sneaked off again—"

"I did not sneak!" Taylor yelped. "Tony!"

Tony's face had plenty of expression now. He looked harried, worried and exasperated. "What's this all about? Mother, you can't mean what you're saying. The kids have been going to the beach all their lives, it's part of their lives, a good part. And Taylor does not sneak."

"Well, it was possibly an unfortunate choice of words. But she did disobey my explicit orders. Taylor is not a child any longer, Tony. She's a young lady."

"She means I get my period," Taylor snapped.

"If you insist on being coarse—"

"What's coarse about that? I just said a fact, that's all."

"Tony, *if* I may be permitted to finish a sentence, it is not a sound idea for a girl Taylor's age to wander on a public beach by herself in the evening. You know there are all sorts of undesirable people frequenting the beaches of Florida and—well, need I go on? It's our duty to protect the girl, since her mother is not here to do it."

"Junie never stopped me from going to the beach," said Taylor. "And neither have you, Tony."

Tony closed his reddened eyes, opened them, fixed his gaze on the fan that revolved about them, stirring the torrid air. "Never thought about it," he said at length. "I suppose my mother's right, Taylor. I just—never thought about it."

"But Tony—"

"And, while we're about it," Grandmother Reddick went on, "I cannot say too strongly how dangerous I consider it for Taylor to sleep out on that hammock the way she does. It's simply asking for trouble."

"What kind of trouble?" Taylor asked grimly.

"Precisely the sort of trouble I've been talking about. You are a young girl, exposing yourself to heaven knows what dangers. If someone approached you on that dock at night, there'd be no one to protect you—"

"Why should anyone approach me on the dock at night?"

"You know, Tony," his mother said, "there's a peculiar kind of—I don't know whether to term it innocence or stupidity—about all of you here. Terrible things happen, and they don't necessarily happen to strangers in newspapers, and the very least you can do is see that your children are protected as much as you are able to protect them. You can't guard against every hazard, but some things you can insist upon. I've tried to reason with Taylor about her imprudence, but I have no effect on her at all, so it's up to you. I have to add that it makes my job here extremely difficult, when I have to go to you to back up my directions."

Job, thought Taylor. Directions. Explicit orders. *I can't love her.* Not even for Tony. She pushed her chair away from the table and started out of the room.

"Taylor, come back," said her father.

"*Please,*" said his mother. "Taylor, come back, *please.* I am attempting to teach the children a few rudimentary manners, and it doesn't help to have you—"

A burst of laughter from Tony cut her short, and Taylor put her hand over her mouth to hide a smile. Tony must've been taking this sort of thing from his mother all his life. Practically forty and still getting etiquette lessons from Mommy. No wonder he'd run away from Massachusetts.

Grandmother, of course, had caught her hidden giggle. She said stiffly, her eyes on Taylor, but speaking to her son, "It's no wonder that child is so rude."

"You just said I wasn't a child," Taylor pointed out.

B.J., who'd been following the conversation with interest, beamed, and Tony threw up his hands, muttering, "Jesus!"

"Tony!" said his mother.

9

"Tony!" shouted Jem, coming in the porch door. "Come out in the skiff, everybody! There's manatees at the back of Wrasse Island! I came back to bring you! Holy cow! I mean, holy sea cow! They're the friendliest things you ever saw, I been petting them and everything. . . . You can see the crisscross marks where they've been hit by outboard motors, it's awful, but they're so great—"

"Where did you come from?" Grandmother Reddick

demanded. "How did you manage to come in that door when you haven't come out of your room?"

"Went out the window," Jem said carelessly. "C'mon everybody, will you? Get some apples, Taylor, we'll feed them. You too, Grandmother. You might never get to see a sea cow in your whole life again. Come *on*!"

"Went out the window—" Grandmother was beginning, but the rest of them were already at the door and running down the dock. Only B.J. turned and said, "You gonna come see, Granny?"

"No," said his grandmother. "I am not going to ride in that little boat, B.J."

"The skiff? There's lots of room."

"B.J., are you coming or aren't you?" Jem hollered. "They won't stay there forever, you know."

But they had remained approximately where Jem had left them. Three manatees. Their long, nearly black bodies, with beaver-shaped tails and walrus faces, moved indolently through the weedy growth. Propelling themselves on their great front flippers in the shallow water, they chewed on young mangrove shoots. Jem cut the motor as he neared them, stood and punted with an oar until the skiff was beside the scarred and gentle beasts.

"Dumbbells," Jem said affectionately. "They don't have sense to get out of the way when they hear a motor coming. Lookit how beat up they are, from blades cutting them."

"They can't move fast enough to get out of the way," Tony said.

"What do you suppose they're doing here?" Taylor asked. "I've never seen manatees in the bay before. Only in rivers, or estuaries."

"That's probably where they came from," Jem said. "The mouth of the river. I sure hope they know their way back. Hold the fort, Tony, I'm going in with them."

He slid over the side of the skiff and swam quietly up to the sea cows. They were in such shallow water that he was able to stand beside them. One rolled over at his touch, seeming to enjoy it when he ran his hands down the great barnacled body. Taylor went in, and B.J. was almost over the side before Tony stopped him.

"Why not?" B.J. said indignantly. "If they can, why can't—"

"Ah, B.J., give me a break, will you? You're too small to be in there with those whales. And I'm tired of arguing. Just look at them, can't you?"

"Well, they aren't *whales.*"

"I was speaking metaphorically."

B.J. didn't challenge that. One of the manatees moved close enough so that he could lean over and pat its head with his small hand, as confidently as he'd have patted Drum. "I could ride on him, I betcha."

"Bet you could, but you aren't going to. You can feed him some of these apples, if you want."

On the way over, Taylor had cut a lot of apples into quarters and she and Jem were feeding the manatees, whose mouths, equipped with flexible ivory-colored short whiskers, sucked in the pieces of fruit with vacuum-like efficiency. B.J., feeling the clutch of the whiskers around his small hand, shrieked with joy. "Tony! Tony . . . he likes me, see? Here, you give him one—"

Taylor, leaning lovingly over one of the manatees, said, "He looks like Hagar, doesn't he, Jem?" She and Jem and B.J. loved Hagar the Horrible, and Tony thought she was right, the creatures did look like the comic-strip Viking, without his helmet.

Watching his children's ecstatic expressions, Tony wondered that they could be part of the lethal link in the chain of evolution. Being human, they were, and yet it was impossible to see them as such.

That evening, because Tony was at home, he and Taylor and Jem had their dinner at eight o'clock. Grandmother and B.J. had eaten their usual sort of food at their usual hour, but Tony prepared seviche, scampi grilled outside so there'd be no odors in the house, a salad of spinach, romaine, sweet onions and mushrooms, his own French bread and a crème caramel. They ate on the dock.

"Oh boy," said Jem, scooping up the last drop of caramel from his dish. "Tony, you're a genius."

"If you and Taylor keep telling me that, I'll end up believing it."

"You better believe it," his son said contentedly. "Why don't you retire and just stay home and cook for us, and we can go sailing and fishing. Maybe we could get a bigger boat and go around the world."

"Don't think I wouldn't like to."

"I think it's too bad," said Jem, "that some people are rich enough so they could stop working but they don't, and other people would like to stop working but aren't rich enough. Maybe I'll rob one of Mr. Howard's banks. Just a little one. A drive-up window, maybe. How much you think we'll need, Tony?"

"I don't like to hear you talk like that, even in fun."

"Okay, Tony," Jem said agreeably. "I wouldn't want to be a robber, anyway. I'd be too scared."

"And I wouldn't really want to stop working. I'd be too bored."

"Comes out even, then."

Tony caught Taylor's wrist as she started to stack the dishes. "Don't do that yet, honey. Let's just the three of us sit here and watch the sunset sky. Let's all agree to live in the moment. Right now, for us, the moment consists of the sun going down over there in the Gulf."

B.J.'s moment was passing unnoticed. He went to bed now, and to sleep, without a mumbling word, at eight o'clock. Without a Daniel Green at the foot of his bed anymore. For Grandmother Reddick, the moment was being lived in the peace and coolness of her room. Days, despite the heat that kept her blotting her neck and brow with tissues, she sat downstairs in front of the color TV set to look at her programs, usually with B.J. beside her, and sometimes Jem or even Taylor. Taylor liked *Sesame Street,* especially Ernie and Bert in their little room at night with the moon shining through the window on Bert's endless efforts to get to sleep and Ernie's innocent methods of thwarting him. ~~But~~ after supper, Grandmother Reddick went upstairs to bathe and retire to a long evening of black and white. It seemed to Taylor that her grandmother almost lived her life through television, even organizing around it the housework that she seemed to love. Tony didn't appear to notice, but she and Jem, in the beginning, had tried to tempt her to share some of the wonders of their island. They'd offered to take her around the bay in the skiff or the Sunfish. To Wrasse Island for picnics. To the beach at sunrise or sunset, in the day to build sand castles, or just to walk and see the birds. Grandmother wasn't too old to do outdoor things. She was lively, physically, and in awfully good health. But she would not go with them anywhere. She just about wouldn't go out of the house, except to the market and back. After a while, they'd stopped asking her. So there she was, living her moment in a TV game show.

And where, and how, just now, at this very second, is Junie living her moment? Taylor wondered. You'd have thought that the longer a person was gone, the less the people left behind would miss her. It wasn't working out that way for Taylor, and she didn't think it was for Tony or her brother. She wouldn't dream of asking them.

10

Somewhere in the midst of the rough, lush, ligneous acres at the back of their house, Taylor wandered with her binoculars, looking at birds. A nice writer had said, "I watch the birds and the birds watch me." Entirely true. You might even say, "I follow the birds and some follow me." A black-whiskered vireo had been flitting from live oak to silk oak to palm to pine, in and out of the underbrush, just a shade behind her since she'd come in here. He kept calling, in his sweet, unvarying, paired phrases. Just to be calling, Taylor told herself, but liked to think he was talking to her. A towhee had started out to keep them company, but dropped back after a minute or two. She'd seen pine and prairie warblers, one prothonotary, and a flutter of yellow-throats. She'd stood for minutes, watching a green heron wading where the bay, at high tide, entered the wood's edge. Now she sat on a fallen palm trunk, her glasses trained on a red-shouldered hawk sitting on a fallen oak bough about fifty feet away. Once he had fixed her with his penetrating gaze, but had not taken alarm at her arrival and seemed intent now on studying the swampy ground beneath him. Waiting for a snake, a crab, a frog, something to stay his never-satisfied hunger. Beautiful, as all hawks are, the red-shouldered was fairly common around here. If, thought Taylor, any bird can be called common around here anymore. If you bulldozed all the trees and covered the land with houses and highways and shopping malls—the apparent aim in Florida—where could the birds find homes?

She brought this rarely common hawk close with her binoculars, lovingly studied the soft rose-barred breast, the scarlet shoulder patches, the intelligent, golden-eyed, sharp-beaked head. He stretched one wing, lazily displaying the translucent tips of his primary feathers. Taylor sighed with a joy so complete it made her vision blur. Then, an arrow speeding from the bow, the hawk was off his perch and raking the ground, so fast that she almost lost him in her glasses and dropped them to her lap to follow his pursuit with her own sharp eyes. It was over in a moment for a small blacksnake, and the hawk winged off, dinner trailing from his talons.

Taylor, scratching her ankles where mosquitoes had got her, rubbing her temple where a wasp had stung her, walked home.

Grandmother and B.J. were at the dining-room table, playing Go Fish. The big new color television was keeping them company, though they seemed not to be paying attention. Taylor felt a shudder of annoyance so familiar by now that she almost ignored it. That was B.J., who had once followed her and Jem from morning till night till at times it got on their nerves. B.J., who had now crawled indoors like a hermit crab in a too-commodious shell. Grandmother Reddick looked up with a greeting as Taylor passed, but B.J., shouting, "There, Granny! Gotcha!" didn't even notice her.

What I wouldn't give, thought Taylor, to have him get on my nerves again.

Upstairs, she went into the bathroom and took a look at her face. There wasn't much to do about wasp stings. She shed her clothes, got into the shower and stood for a long time under the cold water, holding her face up to the spray. Then she dabbed baking soda on the swelling, not expecting it to help, and went to her room and lay down, letting water evaporate from her body. That, for a while, made her feel cool.

She loved this eight-sided room of hers that was like

a tower topping the house. There were bird posters on the four walls, and through the four large windows she could see over the bay, down the bay, over the back acres, to the Gulf of Mexico. She'd got in the habit of keeping the place in some sort of order. In the old days, her bed had been made once a week when she changed the linen. Clothes had piled up on the floor, on hooks, on chairs, until she got around to taking them down to the laundry room. Books and papers. Bird books. Novels Sandy had pressed upon her. Crayons, charcoal, drawing boards, pen and ink. Drawings she had done of various birds at rest or in flight. Drawings of crabs, which she found oddly beautiful. Ghost crabs, stone crab, and the deeply blue blue crab. Drawings of lizards and air plants. Notebooks with her life lists of birds at varying stages of her own life, and the up-to-date one of one hundred and forty-seven birds, all Florida sightings. Her accumulation of shells, not nearly as spectacular as Junie's but her own. (Junie had shelled in the Caribbean, that time when Tony had taken her on a trip. The only time Taylor could remember that they'd gone away, just the two of them together. Junie had brought her back a great pink conch shell that she used for a doorstop. That must've been a wonderful time they'd had, snorkeling and scuba diving among the coral reefs, sailing and fishing. Junie had even got Tony to dance with her. But they'd never gone again. Tony said the trip had cost too much.) But this room—didn't she have it kind of in order now? Books, shells, drawings, notebooks, stacked in piles. Practically nothing for the laundry room. Bed made, even if she was lying on it, getting it rumpled in the daytime. In some of her notebooks she had poems she'd copied:

Stupidity Street
I saw with open eyes
Singing birds sweet
Sold in the shops
For the people to eat,
Sold in the shops of
Stupidity Street.

I saw in vision
The worm in the wheat,
And in the shops nothing
For people to eat;
Nothing for sale in
Stupidity Street.

She wondered if Ralph Hodgson, the poet, had guessed that one day the whole world would be paved with Stupidity Streets.

There were verses she'd tried to write. A hokku:

A knitting of knots
Beside the purling ocean
They stitch the white sand.

Sandy had loved it and said it should be submitted to a magazine, but shy Taylor wouldn't do that.

She kept her room fairly tidy because if she didn't, Grandmother Reddick would march right in and straighten up according to her standards. Taylor had asked Tony to ask his mother not to come into her room and clean and make the bed and carry her clothes down to the laundry room and, though she hadn't said this, *pry*. Her father said it was her problem and she'd have to deal with it. She didn't have the nerve to ask her grandmother to stay out and had settled for trying to keep the place so there'd be no need to come in. But who knew? Short of putting a little stick against the door, or a hair where it would be displaced by poking fingers, she didn't know how to make sure that her room was really her own. She was not going to leave sticks and hairs around like a spy. Suppose she found out that her grandmother was still coming in, checking things, touching things? She still wouldn't have the nerve to say, *Will you please stay out of my room. . . .*

When she'd asked Jem if he minded having his privacy invaded, he'd turned out his hands and said, "Makes no difference to me. Since I can't have my aquariums I'm hardly ever in the room anyway except to sleep. I don't care if it looks like pig alley or the Marine barracks."

Taylor touched the side of her face, wincing a little. Could a wasp bite poison a person enough so she could put off starting school?

School. Three days away.

Well, there it was. She'd contrived to push the whole

matter to the back of her mind for weeks, but here it came, flopping to the foreground, demanding recognition. In the village school, where she'd gone till now, she'd been happy. She liked studying, liked her teachers, liked being able to bike to and from the school, which was small, as everything in the village was small, and surrounded by palms and acacias and Brazilian peppers and bougainvillea vines. When they'd built the new high school on the mainland a couple of years before, they'd gone through the land with bulldozers and removed all the trees. They'd erected a horrible stainless-steel-and-glass complex of buildings, spread a huge parking lot to one side and playing fields to the other. Somewhere approximately in the middle of what was now the faculty parking area there had been a huge old slash pine in which an eagle pair had nested for twenty years, returning each fall to add a stick or two, raise a chick or two. Where had the eagles fled to when they'd returned to find their tree, their nest, the home they'd always known, vanished? Where did all the creatures go who were crowded out of their homes by human beings—so much greedier and stronger than they were?

"Damn," she said aloud. "Damn everything—"

High school was going to mean not only that awful building, but hundreds of strangers and obligatory sports unless you could get a doctor's excuse, which she was sure she could not. She loathed sports. She could swim and run and dive and climb like a wild thing, but she did not want to be on a *team* of anything.

"Blast!"

She got up and pulled on shorts and a shirt. She looked into the closet, where her new school clothes were hanging. Four dresses, three skirts, several blouses, two sweaters, two pairs of shoes including deckers with heels that had seemed to her, in the store, irresistible. If it had not been for Grandmother Reddick, this stuff would not be in the closet. She'd have got up Monday morning with "nothing to wear." A couple of old skirts and some blouses. Two or three pairs of jeans that were getting kind of small. All pretty tacky. When Grandmother Reddick had asked about the matter of school clothes, Taylor had said she guessed she had enough.

"I can imagine what that means," Grandmother had said. Taylor, confident that her grandmother knew every stitch in the closet and in all the drawers, didn't reply.

"What do you plan to wear when school begins?" Grandmother had persisted.

"I hadn't thought about it. I better get something. We can go to the Women's Exchange."

"I don't buy people's discards."

"It's okay, I'll go by myself. Junie gets lots of our things, and hers, at the Women's Exchange. Nothing's dirty, you know. It's all very clean, and you get good buys."

"I do not understand you people at all. A Lowestoft tureen, a set of fruit knives and forks with gold handles, and secondhand clothing. It's preposterous."

"Junie isn't very clothes conscious."

"You don't say. Well, you and Jem and I will go into town and get you both something decent to start school in."

"Jem won't want to. He doesn't need anything anyway. He's just going to the village like always."

"*As* always. I want you both to have new clothes, Taylor."

"I'm not sure Tony can afford it."

"It'll be my treat."

With poor grace, Taylor agreed. Whether or not you wished to be treated, Grandmother Reddick treated you when she had a mind to. So here she was with a closetful of new threads and no way to head off Monday.

Jem, as she'd known he would, had declined the treat altogether and wouldn't be budged. Jem unbudgeable was tougher than Grandmother Reddick determined. Taylor was not sure, even watching him, how he managed to dodge her demands if they didn't suit him, and emerge every time unrebuked, unreproached. Maybe it was something very complicated—like, for instance, Jem was a psychological genius. Or maybe it was something exceedingly simple. Like—Jem was a boy. In Grandmother Reddick's world, what more did a person need to be?

11

Taylor sat on a window seat, looking out at the woods, chin on her hands, scowling at the future. Then the world brightened as Sandy came upstairs, calling, "You there, Taylor?"

"Where else?"

Coming into the room, Sandy thrust forward a small porcelain vase with three passionflowers in it. "Did you notice the passionflower bush at our place is in bursting bloom? Well, it is. I cut these for your grandmother. I think we ought to pay her little attentions, since she's doing so much for you. And she said, 'Oh, aren't you sweet, dear, but do be sure there are no insects lurking in the petals.' I mean, she didn't even *look* at them. I think she's great. So predictable and funny. I know, I know—it's different when you live with it. But look at the bright side. She doesn't drink. She *doesn't,* does she?"

"Oh, Sandy."

"So that's a bright aspect." Sandy dropped into a chair that still had one of Junie's old covers on it and said, "Poof! Wonder when is the heat going to let up. You people really should get air conditioning. Central. You know what I'm trying to figure out, Taylor? I'm trying to figure out why it is that my father doesn't appear to be aware that his wife is bombed most of the time. Do you suppose he's making the best of it, or doesn't care, or *really* doesn't notice? I know he's an island entirely surrounded by himself, but wouldn't you think a message would get through from time to time? A smoke signal, a drumbeat—*something*?"

"Have you ever tried talking to her yourself?"

"Yes. Two or three times, and it's always the same. First she looks as if I'd slapped her, then she starts crying. She cries and cries. It's terrible. Then she has a glassful of straight room-temperature vodka, and afterward doesn't ever remember that anything got said at all. Vodka is not smell-less. It stinks."

"I'm so sorry, Sandy."

"I know you are. I can't think what I'd do without

you. But what I started out to say, actually, is that having a vigilant grandmother is not the absolute bottom of the jar, especially as she may be going away one of these days."

"What gives you that idea?"

"Well, there's at least a chance that Junie will come back, or Granny will get fed up with all of you and split."

"Nope. No chance. She has a New England conscience, Tony says. That kind doesn't give up the ship."

"Like the old Nantucket whalers, going down with it. What's wrong with your eye?"

"Wasp bite. I'm hoping to be bedridden by Monday."

"You won't be. I do hope the swelling goes down. You want to be a credit to us, your first day in the new and larger world ahead of us."

"It would be idle to deny that I care for that and that alone."

"Now come on, Taylor. Don't be difficult. It's one of the things I want to talk to you about. School."

"I *don't* want to talk about it. I'm living a day at a time and I've got two and a half days left."

"I've decided we should wear dresses, not pants. For a while, anyway. And we'll bike over, not take that bus. It's only about three miles."

"Biking's okay. And I have to wear dresses. Grandmother Reddick bought me some and she says I can't wear pants to school. We got the dresses retail."

"No kidding. Can I see?" She walked over and looked in the closet. "My. How ladylike."

Taylor nodded indifferently.

"What's such a downer about high school, Taylor? There'll be lots of the same kids we went to school with here, and you're not sociable anyway. You just have to be unsociable three miles farther from home. Amanda says some of the teachers are pretty good. They'll have to be Einsteins, for her to say that. Amanda may be a social nonstarter—"

"Like me?" Taylor interrupted.

"There's a difference. She doesn't *want* to be that way. She sometimes acts as if she's ripe for the cooky farm, but Amanda is very very bright. So I expect some of the teachers will be good, and that'll be a plus. You know, since that Alexander made his escape, she's been in a constant state of acedia."

"What's acedia?" Taylor asked obediently.

"Spiritual apathy. Actually, it's sloth, one of the seven deadly sins. Manifested by a total indifference to surroundings. Also indolence, and in Amanda's case crying spells. She asked me if I thought if maybe she'd shaved her legs and her armpits when Alexander shaved his beard maybe he wouldn't have left her."

"Some feminist."

"That's what I thought."

"What did you tell her?"

"Well, I said he was going to Princeton whether she did or did not shave, and I thought she ought to have the courage of her principles even if it does look like she's walking around on a couple of minks."

"What a comfort you must be to her."

"I do try, really. I think she needs *bracing*. She's so glum and sorry for herself. I can't understand why that shrink Dr. Borden isn't doing either one of them any good. I don't understand at all why Dan keeps going. Over a year now and they haven't exchanged a syllable."

"You said yourself he must be helping in some way, or Dan wouldn't keep going to him."

"I suppose." Sandy sighed. "One dipso, one tyrant, two head cases. What am *I*?"

Fat, thought Taylor. There must be a reason for that.

"I'm plump, of course," said Sandy. "And nobody's plump for no reason. But somehow it doesn't seem to bother me. Maybe *that* should bother me? Isn't it getting to be lunchtime? Have you had yours?"

Taylor grinned. "No. Let's go down and get something." She looked at the clock. "Grandmother will be taking her nap. Let's go."

In the living room, B.J. was sitting by himself in front of the television, watching a documentary about the Volga River. Taylor went over and stood between him and the set.

"Taylor," he said mildly, moving his head so he could see, "you're in front of my program."

"You get up from that sofa and go outside and find something to do in the fresh air, you hear me?"

"No, I want to—"

Taylor turned the picture off. "Get! Take your little boat and row out to the sandbar and tell me if you see any blue crabs. We could go crabbing after Sandy and I have a bite."

B.J. hesitated a moment, then smiled. "Okay. Where's Jem?"

"I don't know. But you can take the boat by yourself. The tide's low."

In the kitchen, Sandy leaned on the windowsill watching as B.J. pushed a little white rowboat into the water, fitted the oars, waited for Drum to jump in with him, looked over his shoulder, and then began pulling for the sandbar.

"Look at him go. He handles a boat almost as well as you or Jem. Where'd he get that cute little thing?"

"Some man at the restaurant gave it to him. It belonged to one of his kids who outgrew it."

"It's darling. Are we really going crabbing?"

"If he finds any. And if you'll help me pick the meat out."

"It isn't at the *top* of my preferred things to do in the afternoon, but okay. I do love crabmeat. What're we having for lunch?"

Taylor peered in the icebox. "There's broccoli soup and some leftover chicken salad."

"Any of Tony's rolls or bread?"

"Yes. And peaches."

"That'll do nicely."

On the porch at the round table they watched as B.J. and Drum stumped over the sandbar. Terns and gulls and pelicans, disturbed by their arrival, circled overhead, settled at the farther end of the bar, rose again, settled again.

"Did I tell you we saw manatees the other day?" Taylor asked, munching on one of Tony's crusty rye rolls. "Over at the back of Wrasse Island."

"You didn't tell me, but Dan found out. He had a fit because Jem didn't take him to see them, too."

"We tried to phone, but your line was busy."

"Oh, Taylor. How you do fib. I mean, it's you talking to me, not Jem and Dan. I know Jem tells these kindly lies to my brother once in a while, to spare his feelings, but you don't have to pull the same stuff with me. Dan follows Jem like a tail, and I can understand why Jem would get tired of it once in a while—"

"But he doesn't. He's devoted to Dan. They're friends."

"So're you and I, but maybe you get tired, too. Of having me around most of the time. I talk so much, and you're a retiring type, and I wouldn't blame you if you got sick of hearing me discuss my family indiscreetly and at length. You never complain about your family."

"I do about my grandmother."

"I don't think you consider her part of the family. But you never say boo about Tony or Junie or any of what went on. And I go on and on and on about everything. No, it wouldn't surprise me if you got weary of my company now and then."

"Well, I don't. Not ever."

"Good. It's to be hoped that the vortexes of our lives remain congruent."

Taylor burst out laughing, sputtering crumbs over the table. "Sorry," she said, brushing them away. "But you are so funny."

"I bet you all got a charge out of seeing the manatees."

"It was marvelous, simply heavenly. Jem read up about them afterward. They're of the order Sirenia, and they're supposed to account for myths about sirens and mermaids. When Christopher Columbus sailed into the West Indies, he wrote in his log, 'We have seen mermaids, and I am sorry to say they are not as beautiful as they are reputed to be.' "

"That's gorgeous! He must've been feeling right horny, to mistake a manatee for a mermaid. Of course, it was a long crossing."

Taylor wondered how her friend could ever for a moment be uncertain of her welcome anywhere. It seemed that even the people who seemed most sure of themselves after all were not, not all the time. Was that a thing to take heart at, or be discouraged by, if you were yourself a retiring type?

B.J. returned to report no sightings of crabs. He sat down, looked the table over and said, "Don't leave crumbs, Taylor. They draw bugs. You and Jem are careless."

"How would you like a poke in the snoot?"

"Well, I'm only saying."

"Don't. One person calling my attention to crumbs is all I need."

"What's the matter with your eye? Did somebody poke you in the snoot?" B.J. was staring at her with delight. "Lookit, Sandy. Her eye's just about closed. Does it hurt?" he asked curiously.

"No."

"But it must, Taylor. You know, you shouldn't go where wasps will sting you."

Feeling her temper slip, Taylor forced a smile. "What do you suggest, B.J.? That I stay in the house all day long looking at television or playing cards?"

"You want to play cards?" he said happily.

Sandy got to her feet. "I'll help you clear up here, Taylor, and then I think I'll whiz back to my part of the forest. Have you started *Catcher in the Rye* yet?"

"No, I haven't," Taylor snapped.

"You really should read it. It's a wonderful book."

"You mean it's the best book you ever read in your entire life last week?"

"Can I help it if there's so much good stuff around to read? Has Jem started anything I left for him?"

"He's reading *Treasure Island* and loving it. Okay?"

After Sandy had gone, Taylor went back upstairs and lay on her bed. All at once she was tired of everybody and everything. B.J. being a prissy little pest, Sandy bugging her about books, and Grandmother Reddick just *being*.

And the wasp bite did hurt.

On the day of the manatees Tony had been almost jolly, but since then he'd slumped back into his detached world of staring silences. Was Tony a victim of acedia?

No. Because he was the least slothful person in the world. Only what about those hours when he was home when he just lay in the hammock, unmoving, unspeaking? Except she didn't think he was being lazy then. She thought he was thinking, furiously. She thought he was furious all the time. There was nothing lazy about that. It took energy to stay angry. Even if someday Junie wanted to come home, how could she return to a person in such a rage? Tony could not be an easy person for a wife to live with. He wasn't easy for his children. And no matter how good a face Grandmother Reddick put on it, could she really *enjoy* being a housekeeper for a man who just about never spoke?

Tony could lie in the hammock whenever he pleased. Taylor missed them, her nights of lying out there at the end of the dock with the sky hanging there like a chandelier and lights from the fishing village across the bay shivering on the dark waters and the sound of mullet leaping and night herons calling and a thin chin of moon resting above Wrasse Island. She'd always been able to sleep out there. Here, in her room, she tossed around on the verge of dreams night after night, never entirely free of the day.

12

On Sunday morning at first light Taylor, in her bathing suit, crept downstairs to her brothers' room with the intention of waking Jem. At the door she hesitated, looking at them with an eye almost maternal.

B.J. slept sprawled on his back, sheet pushed away from his slender brown body. His mouth was open a little and small snorts issued from it. The floor fan, turning its face from boy to boy, didn't reach his head, which was moist with sweat. Drum lay with his head on his paws, close to B.J.'s bed. No one could see Jem's head when he slept. Even in the hottest weather he clasped a pillow over it. Taylor thought it must be a security measure, but he'd been doing it since he was a little boy so it had nothing to do with his mother's absence. Funny that if his head was covered, he didn't mind the rest of himself being naked and coverless. Like an ostrich. In the curve of his legs slept their big cat, Tut. The animals clearly belonged, or gave their loyalty to, the boys. Taylor liked them, but left to herself would not have kept a domestic pet. The Dobkins had a parrot they'd brought up in their boat from Cozumel, and though it had a cage it spent most of its time walking around on the furniture, nibbling tables, chewing up plants. It had a pretty good vocabulary and was extremely handsome. The first time Sandy had seen it, she'd decided that Taylor, too, should have a parrot. "Anyone who's crackers over birds the way you are should have a bird of her very own, and if you like I'll speak to your parents about it." But Taylor had laughed and said please don't. A bird in a cage, even a bird that didn't stay in its cage, had no place in her life. Calling her crackers over them was all right, but what she felt was not that. Her feeling for birds was a passion, something that would never change. She would find a world without birds a place she could not endure. You didn't tell people, even someone as close to her as Sandy was, a thing like that. Maybe especially not Sandy, since she was so curious, so determined to follow up on any observation that caught her interest. Saying I couldn't endure a world without birds, Taylor thought, would catch Sandy's interest like a hook. "What if they all disappeared, actually literally disappeared?" Sandy would say. "Then what? You going to swim out in the Gulf and never come back? What would you do, I mean really *do,* if you woke up one morning and found the birds forever gone, from all over the planet, not even an egg left you could sit on and hatch?" Taylor wasn't altogether sure that in that case she would *not* swim out in the Gulf, toward Mexico and a deep grave. It was not a matter she'd give Sandy a chance to quiz her about.

She leaned over Jem and shook his shoulder gently. "Jem. Jem, wake up," she whispered.

He pulled the pillow off his head and stared at her with wide-awake eyes. He woke the way his cat did. Sandy had once said that some people wake up awake and some people wake up asleep and never the twain should try for a meaningful relationship. Jem woke awake.

"Yeah? Whatcha want?"

"Come over to the Gulf with me, Jem. We can see the sun rise."

"It rises over the bay."

"You know what I mean."

"Okay. Right with you."

B.J. and Drum slept on undisturbed, but Tut rose, stretched his front legs, his back legs one at a time, yawned and got down from the bed. He bounded toward the kitchen, tail high, confident that Jem would follow and provide. Which he did. Then he and Taylor went out to the garage, swung onto their bikes and set off for the beach.

At this hour, with the dark waning, there was a faint freshening of the air, though they knew that in a little while the temperature would be back in the nineties, as it had been for weeks. People said it was the hottest summer they'd ever known, even people who'd lived in Florida all their lives. Taylor felt really sorry for her grandmother, having to do her rescue work in the hottest summer anyone could recall.

"I wonder if we should've left a note for Grandmother?" she said.

"I did."

"Oh."

Thoughtfulness, thought Taylor, comes naturally to Jem. I wish it did to me.

"Do you realize," she said to her brother, "that in exactly a year B.J. will be old enough to start kindergarten? A garden of children, that's what that means. Isn't that nice? *Answer* me, Jem."

"Yes, it's nice."

"And then Grandmother can go back to Massachusetts."

"I guess."

"I'm sure she'll want to, don't you think? She's always talking about New England. The grooviest grove on God's green earth, New England. And she hates Florida and doesn't like us, except Tony."

"She's crazy about B.J."

"She's crazy about this kid she's turned him into. A mushroom-colored TV-watching moron. I much preferred him when he was a savage. At least he was *doing* something then."

"Like gluing the pages of your bird book together?"

"Even that. Anything to have him back the way he used to be."

"Do you mind if we don't talk about it?"

"But you *never* want to talk about it."

"Because there isn't any point in talking. Things are how they are and maybe they'll change and maybe they won't but you and me talking adds up to zilch and it just makes me jumpy. I hate being jumpy."

They pedaled on in silence to the beach, laying their bikes at the edge of the sand.

"C'mon," Jem said. "Let's run!" and he was off down the beach. Taylor, with longer legs, was able to catch up with him. For a mile they ran side by side, stopped at a fallen palm trunk they'd labeled their checkpoint, wheeled and ran back to their starting point where Jem, without pausing, splashed into the waves, hurled himself flat and was away with his swift smooth crawl.

He stopped before long. The waves were too high for swimming, so for a while they bodysurfed toward the beach. But as the sun's rays turned the eastern sky to cherry-gold they stood in water to their waists, just looking. Theirs was a barrier island—a narrow key that ran parallel to the mainland and was connected to it at each end by a drawbridge. From this island a phenomenon could be seen each morning. The sun, rising in the east where it could be expected to, shed its light on great clouds piled in the west, giving the effect of two sunrises. While the eastern sky glowed with Oriental splendor, massy clouds in the west became radiant with a rose reflection, so that the waters of the Gulf, and the sand where the waves receded, were washed with a glossy coral brightness.

You have to be up early in the morning to see it, thought Taylor, lying back on the water to float. The waves took her body and rocked it, lifting and lowering, turning her from side to side. High against the now-blue expanse of sky a few frigate birds rode the thermals, scarcely moving their wings. At the water's edge a company of pharaonic ibises walked sedately, their long curved bills seeking crustaceans. Once they'd been Egyptian gods and now they were common shorebirds, but it had not affected their dignity. Tut had been a god, too, in ancient Egypt, but took his present role without loss of pride. Only human beings, thought Taylor, want to be, or to worship, gods.

On the crescent sandbar a great aggregation of birds mingled peaceably. At this hour there was no one to disturb them, except for Taylor and her brother and a couple walking far down the beach. A tremendous amount of fishing was going on among the birds. So many shiners were in the water that as they schooled in their thousands, some bumped into Jem and Taylor.

"Look, Taylor," Jem said. She glanced over to find

him standing again, smiling with pleasure at a school of mullet that streaked past just below the surface of the water, riding the waves like small silver surfers. Here and there a mullet leaped, once, sometimes two or three times. Wonderful leapers, they seemed to hang in a tinsel shimmy before plopping back into the waves.

"Just joy, that's what it is," said Jem, as one leaped and splashed into the water and leaped again, only feet away from him. There was a theory that mullet leaped to escape larger fish, but Jem wouldn't buy it. "Notice there aren't any big fish around this morning," he said to Taylor. "They just know how to live, these dudes. Swim, and jump for joy, and if you get caught, so what—you've had yourself a time."

Sandy had once said she had read a definition of joy. It said that contentment is a solid, happiness is a liquid, and joy is a gas. She quoted this now to Jem.

"Hey, hey—neat," he said, and dove into a huge wave that loomed toward them. Taylor took it floating and went on watching the birds at their fishing. A great company of terns frolicked overhead, nimble as spirits, turning their heads down from time to time to study the water, then plunging and emerging in swift, delicate, nearly always successful maneuvers. They took only the tiniest fish, which they then tossed into the air and caught, like a person tossing and catching peanuts. Terns were chalky white, with black wing tips, and they called their short shrill note unwearyingly. Pelicans, so much larger than even the big royal tern, shot into the water, sending it fountaining around them as they hit. They did not fly off with a catch but rode the waves, shaking their loose-skinned bills to get the catch in swallowing position, meanwhile fending off gulls that pirated what they could where they could, even out of a pelican's bill if possible.

"I could never live anywhere except by the water," she said to her brother. "Never."

"As soon as I get old enough, I'm going to live on it."

"Doing what?"

"Maybe I'll captain a charter boat during the season, in the Bahamas or like that. I could deliver boats from the north for rich people who don't want to bring them down themselves. That sort of thing. Until I make enough money to get a sloop of my own. After that I'll just bum around the world. You can always earn enough in port to keep yourself and a boat and a cat."

"No college?"

"No way. What for? I can learn to navigate without going to college, and I already like to read. What else could they teach me?"

"You're just going to bum around on a boat all your life?"

"Yup."

"No wife, no family?"

"Nope."

Think of it. Ten years old and he already knew what he was going to do until he died. Taylor had no idea what her future would be, what she would do with it. Be an ornithologist, maybe, if she could afford the training, if there were enough birds left to study when she got old enough to study them. What she would have liked was to be free to wander the world just looking at them. She'd have to be rich for that, and she knew she would never be rich.

"Maybe I could crew for you," she said to Jem.

"Great. We'll split the watches and the cooking," he said and went into another wave.

The couple, who'd been walking toward them for a long time, stopped a little way up the beach and put their arms around each other, straining close, as if there were no way to get close enough. Their lips met and they stood there, unmoving, except that once in a while they swayed a little. They were close enough so that Taylor could see they were teenagers. She didn't know how she knew, but something about their bodies made them very young, not possibly in their twenties.

Jem glanced the direction she was staring at, shrugged and lay back on the water, hands beneath his head. "Bet I could just float this way to Yucatan."

"I guess," Taylor said absently.

Once, her mother had told her that the day would come when someone's very touch would make her go up in flames. She thought those two, melded together in a kiss, indifferent to anything outside themselves, were burning. They were in a fever of love. Anyway, a fever of longing. She was nearly fourteen and had not known the slightest rise in her temperature at the sight or touch of another human being. To date, of course, no one had ever indicated that he'd like to walk on the beach with her, much less stand embraced and lovesick on the sand for endless minutes. She supposed it would happen someday, but it looked like being a long time yet. Unless love was a sniper and hit without warning. Love, or desire.

Had Amanda and Alexander clutched and kissed and burned that way? Had they made it together or hadn't they? From listening to them that crazy day there'd be no way of telling. But it was said that few girls got out of high school these days still virgins. What am I getting into, she thought, starting high school?

She did a quick surface dive and swam along the sandy floor of the sea, wishing she were a fish.

13

Early Monday morning, Sandy telephoned Taylor to say she'd be leaving by bicycle in five minutes and would Taylor please be waiting at the top of her driveway. "That way we won't waste any time."

"Swell."

"Oh, cheer up, Taylor. I'm looking forward to it. We all need change."

"I hate change."

"You're beginning to sound like your father. I'd watch that, if I were you."

Taylor took a look at herself in the pier glass by the door.

"You look charming," said Grandmother Reddick who was, as always, fully dressed even at this hour. Junie sometimes didn't get out of her nighty till noon. Taylor glanced around the living room, absorbed its trim and orderly look that was beginning to feel familiar.

"The slipcovers are really nice, Grandmother," she said. "In fact, everything looks nice."

Grandmother Reddick's eyes widened slightly, but she covered her surprise with a smile. "That skirt and blouse are lovely on you, and your hair is simply beautiful."

"Thank you for the things."

Her grandmother sighed. "I wish you didn't feel you had to go on thanking me, but I suppose you can't help it."

B.J. shot out of his room, followed by Drum. Taylor noticed that her grandmother did not protest the dog's presence. Compromises all around, she thought, and they weren't necessary only in marriage.

"Where's Jem?" B.J. demanded. "He's not in bed."

"He's gone to school," Taylor said. Gone to her school, the village school, going as she had gone for so many years, a short way from home. Jem had left early, to see his friends. Maybe Sandy could thrive on change, but all Taylor wanted was what she already knew. And in that she guessed she was like her father.

"Why can't I go to school?" B.J. was asking. "I wanna go to school, too!"

"Next year," said Taylor and her grandmother together.

"I don't wanna wait till next year! I'm gonna go to school today! I'm gonna get dressed and follow you, Taylor!"

"Okay. But I expect you'll be put in jail if you do."

"Granny!"

"Taylor's making a joke," said Grandmother Reddick in an unamused voice. "It's a pity they don't have a nursery school in the village."

"I don't wanna go to a nursery with babies!" B.J. screamed. "I wanna go to a regular school!"

"Would you like pancakes for breakfast?" Grandmother Reddick asked, and Taylor, calling good-bye over her shoulder, slipped outside.

Sandy was already waiting, and as they started across the bridge to the mainland, she said, "We have to ride the bus after today."

"Why?"

"My father says it's dangerous for us to bike. In fact, he was threatening to drive us to school himself."

"That's avoiding danger?"

"I know. I talked him out of it for today, but boy if it pours this aft, the way it's been doing every day, he'll have all kinds of reasons for saying he told me so. And it probably will. Rain. Do you mind if we take the bus?"

"No."

"You're the grooviest traveling companion a girl ever had—I want to be sure you know that."

"Go travel with somebody else."

"Oh, cut it out, Taylor. It's a shame, though. You'd be very pretty if you didn't have this cheerless fizz."

"Sandy, I am *not* cheerless. I mean, I am, but that's not the problem. I'm nervous. You may like change but I absolutely hate it."

"Well, I guess you can't help that," Sandy said compassionately. "Maybe you'll have a ball today and everything will seem different—"

I don't want a ball, Taylor thought. I just want— What she wanted was to stay home with B.J. and Jem and never see anybody else except Sandy. And Tony, of course. Since there was no way of getting what she wanted, what was the point in thinking about it? There wasn't even any point in being nervous, except you didn't stop feeling something just because there was no point to it.

"My poor mother," Sandy was saying. "She can't ever do *any*thing she wants. I mean, in her own way."

"What happened?"

"Well, last night we were all sitting in the living room, looking at the telly, except Amanda. She's disfigured by a cold sore so it gives her an excuse to stay upstairs. She practically had hysterics about going to school this morning because of the cold sore but of course he made her go. Why is it that for some people *every*thing works against them? For instance, I would gladly assume

Amanda's cold sore for her, just to spare her the agony of appearing with it in public—and for her it will be agony where for me it would be just a nuisance. Actually, of course, she's luckier than the rest of us in lots of ways. Slim, and with these legs clear up to her shoulders. What I wouldn't give for nice long legs and a skinny bod. But Amanda never counts her blessings. She goes over her misfortunes like a tax accountant. What was my point? I started out to tell you something."

"About your mother."

"Oh yes. Well, there we were, looking at the Sunday night movie, and pretty often my mother falls asleep during it but suddenly I noticed him noticing her so I noticed her too, and she was staring at the ceiling and counting on her fingers and anyone could see she had some plan ticking, so he says in that frostbitten way he has, 'What are you thinking?' I really do not think people should ask other people what they're thinking. If they're thinking, then that's what they're doing. Thinking. Not telling. If they want to tell, they'll tell."

Taylor, who frequently asked Tony or Jem what they were thinking, made a nowhere noise and said, "What was your mother planning? Did you find out?"

"The poor thing was trying to give a party. For Amanda. To make up for losing Alexander. She was working out on her fingers who to ask. What she wanted was to give a Labor Day party for Amanda's school chums. That's how she put it. Why she doesn't dig it that Amanda doesn't have school chums will be the subject of our next lecture. Anyway—she wanted to make it a sort of kids-on-up bash. Everybody from B.J.'s age on up, including your grandmother because she's never met her—"

She's never asked to meet her, Taylor thought, but without rancor. The Howards, who had the Reddick children at their house with and without invitations all the time, had never invited Tony or Junie to one of their big parties. Taylor didn't know for sure why this was, but supposed it had to do with Tony's being a cook and Mr. Howard this important banker. Of course, the last thing Tony or Junie longed for was to be swept into the Howards' social circle, so it came out even.

Turning into the long street leading to the high school, Taylor's spirits shriveled and sank.

"So what happened?" she said, trying hard to be interested in what Sandy was telling her.

"It's turned into a party for the banking community, of course. Catered, since the latest in our parade of peons has slipped bondage. Amanda will of course still be allowed to invite these mysterious school chums and your grandmother's going to be asked, but B.J. is out. And of course also it is not my mother's party anymore. I don't know, Taylor. I've been reading this book on feminists of the nineteenth century, and the more I read the more I think things haven't progressed much. I suppose you have to count sexual freedom—there's plenty of that now, but I'm not sure how much that advances the cause. *Basically*, men are still running the show. Some girls do refuse to get married, if that's progress. And some of them won't take their husband's name if they do, but what's the point to that? You keep your maiden name, it's still some *man's* name, isn't it? If I ever get married, I'm going to ask my mate to pick a name out of a hat and we'll use that."

"Why should he pick it out? Why not you?"

"We'll both pick it out. That way it won't be either of our old ones. One of those women—the nineteenth-century feminists—was named Sojourner Truth. I think that is the topmost marvelous name I ever heard, and she made it up herself. She was a black *and* a feminist, and it was before the Civil War. How's that for courage, huh? She said, in one of her speeches, *I wanted to tell you a mite about Woman's Rights, and so I came out and said so. I am sittin' among you to watch; and every once and awhile I will come out and tell you what time of night it is.* Did you ever *hear* anything so marvelous? Maybe my husband and I will be Sandra and So-and-So Sojourner-Truth. With a hyphen. Just the same, you can't tell me that women have really advanced much since Sojourner Truth's day, except for a member of the Board here and there, or a token congressperson. Look around, Taylor, and see who's the sachem and who's the slave. Most women don't really have any *self.* They're all planets, circling some man."

Grandmother, thought Taylor, circles Tony. Probably when her husband was alive she revolved around him and her little boy, Tony. Who's grown up to think he has a solar right to be at the center of things, just like Mr. Howard. Mr. Howard boiled like a sunspot where Tony shed a sort of gentle light most of the time. But there they were, always in the center and sure they belonged there.

"I think women want to be planets," she said.

"Not all of them. Your mother knew when to stop revolving and spin off on her own."

Leaving behind her three kids flopping around on their own, Taylor thought, but really couldn't fix her thoughts on Tony and Junie this morning. She was fixed on what lay ahead of her now. Four years of high school. She hadn't even got there and already her stomach was sick.

"I think I'll go home, Sandy," she said, pulling to the side of the road. "I can't go through with this."

Sandy stopped beside her. She put out a hand and patted Taylor's back, the way you'd gentle a baby. "Why do you insist on anticipating how you're going to feel? Just take it a day at a time. Or an hour. A minute, if that's all you can manage. You'll be okay, I promise. They say we spend fifteen thousand hours in school, not counting college, and you've already got more than half behind you. You can skip college, if you want to. Look at it that way. Besides, I need you, so do it for me."

"Okay," Taylor said on a shuddering sigh. They pushed off again, Sandy following. Making sure I don't escape, Taylor thought, and had to smile, just a little.

From cars, from buses, on bikes and on roller skates and on foot, students and teachers streamed toward the high school building. Taylor and Sandy locked their bicycles in a long row of racks provided for the purpose, and walked inside.

A loudspeaker blatted instructions, telling people where to go so as to figure out where they went from there. She and Sandy turned out to have the same homeroom, with a young teacher named David Gamble who had the girls gaping. Tall, with a soft voice and a face to make daydreams by, he was going to be their mathematics as well as homeroom teacher. He was also, he informed them, going to coach girls' soccer.

"That does it," Sandy whispered to Taylor. "I always knew it would happen like this. I shall go out for soccer, and naturally I'll have to get the Scarsdale diet book and commence early-morning jogging. You can come with me."

"I'm not motivated to jog. You're on your own."

"You mean you can look at him and say that?"

"Hush!" said a girl behind them. "He's *talking.*"

Mr. Gamble released them shortly to go to their first class. For Taylor, physical geography, and for Sandy, of all things, Latin. "Latin," she explained to Taylor, "is a dead language, and presently all Latin teachers will be dead too. I want to take this chance to study with one of the last of a species."

The corridors were thronged with moving bodies. The loudspeaker, going at full volume to compete with hundreds of young voices, gave instructions about lunchroom schedules and conduct, about special study clubs, about a morning assembly called not for today but for next week, the Tuesday after Labor Day. They sweltered. There was air conditioning in this school, unlike that in the village. But keeping it at the federally required temperature, and adding body heat from so many bodies, had people yawning and sweating before the day had really begun. In the village school, windows would be open and there'd be fans going, and trees outside the old building would be absorbing heat and moisture. Around this place they hadn't left a tree standing. Pretty soon, in Florida, the only place left to find grass or trees would be graveyards and golf courses.

"I hate air conditioning," Taylor said crossly, thinking again about the eagles coming back to find their slash pine forever gone from the treeless landscape.

"I like it when it works. This is horrible. Let's go into the john for a sec."

The girls' rest room was crowded, ringing with conversation and laughter, with shrieks of greeting. There was a faint odor of pot. Looking around, Taylor saw only a group of older girls, juniors or seniors, who were smoking ordinary cigarettes while they discussed summer conquests and defeats.

". . . we went to the French Riviera and I but really got into French boys—"

". . . the other way around, surely?"

". . . I think I'm engaged. Anyway, my *mother* certainly thinks I am—"

". . . and I had a lifeguard, but he got away—"

Taylor had managed to reach the mirror and was deciding that her hair *was* nice, even though this sort of no-color blond, when she saw, reflected, Amanda Howard making for the group, which by the look of it, Taylor decided, was probably A Group. Possibly even The Group. There always was one, in every school. Amanda was holding the fingers of one hand lightly to her face. Trying to cover the cold sore, poor thing, thought Taylor, then winced as Amanda's clear voice rang out, "Hi, everybody! Speaking of fellas, my guy is off to Princeton, wouldn't you know!"

A few of the girls looked at her languidly without speaking, but one dark gleaming beauty fixed her with a dark gleaming eye and said distinctly, "And just *how* should *we* know *that*?" She stared a moment at Amanda, whose face flooded with color; the girl turned and said, "Well, I must be off."

Sandy grabbed Taylor's hand and yanked her toward the door. Outside, they stood a moment, looking at each other miserably. In a shaky voice, Sandy said, "You know, Taylor, I think I can understand most things human beings are driven to do, or to be. If you read a lot you get this broad understanding. But such a *point*less piece of cruelty. That I can't understand, not in any way. That—that bitch is the sort of person who makes me want to wreak vengeance. She's also the kind you can't reach to wreak it on. Poor Amanda. She breaks my heart, you know? Oh well—" She took a deep breath. "See you at lunch."

When Sandy had walked quickly away, Taylor turned and moved slowly in the direction she supposed her physical geography room was located in, wondering why a girl who looked like that would have any need to humiliate Amanda, with her cold sore and her poor little attempt to "be a part." You'd think somebody who looked like that girl could even afford to be kind. She found the right room and took a seat, feeling sad but not at all frightened. So the weeks of queasiness and uneasiness and at times downright terror had been unnecessary. And Sandy, as usual, was right. There was no point in figuring how you were going to feel until you were feeling it.

This geography teacher put her in mind of Grandmother Reddick. She spent most of the class hour calling the roll, making everyone stand and pronounce names "clearly and distinctly, so that I will not mispronounce. To mispronounce a person's name is an affront of which I do not wish to be guilty." She advised them, clearly and distinctly, what the school's policy was as to tardinesses or absences. Drawing and quartering? Taylor thought, yawning with her mouth shut. The teacher went on to describe her own policy as to heads on desks. Hanging? Taylor wondered. She was paying no attention at all, and wondered if she ever would. At her other school she'd been a pretty good student, but this day was not beginning well. . . .

She jerked her head up as the bell rang, glanced guiltily at the teacher, who was eyeing another miscreant. Gathering her books, she stood, pulled her skirt away from sweaty legs and trudged on to the next class.

When they came out of the building that afternoon, it was pouring. "Damn," said Sandy. "I knew it. I *knew* it. He'll be right again."

"What difference does it make?"

"It just annoys me, that's all."

"Sandy!" A man with a huge black umbrella stood on the steps. "Your father sent me to pick you up."

"Gee, thanks, Mr. Brinkerhoff. Taylor, this is Mr. Brinkerhoff, from the bank. This is my friend, Taylor Reddick. We'll have to wait for Amanda."

"Your sister is already at home."

"She is?"

Sandy and Taylor exchanged glances. I'll bet, thought Taylor, she split right after that awful little scene. Amanda's skin was cruelly thin.

"We have bikes here, Mr. Brinkerhoff," Sandy said, her voice dull. "I don't see how we can leave them."

"That's all right. Your father told me to take the station wagon so as to fit them in."

"Thinks of everything, doesn't he?"

Taylor asked to be let out at the top of her driveway. "Don't try to get the bike out," she said to Mr. Brinkerhoff. "I'll pick it up at Sandy's."

"Are you sure I shouldn't take you to your door?" he asked.

"Oh, no. I love the rain." She mimed through the

closed car window to Sandy, "Call me, okay?" then turned and walked down the long shell drive. The rain let up a little, and down the bay you could see that the sun was already shining. Summer rain on this coast of Florida was capricious. It might be pouring on the village while sunlight blazed on the beach. You could stand in sunshine and watch a curtain of rain sweep toward you over the Gulf. Afternoons, in summer, a pageant of rumbling clouds trundled up most days, and gaudy displays of lightning. A show that often came to nothing, but other times made rivers of the highways and turned the bottom of their drive to a lake. Today wind tossed the feathery heights of Australian pines, creaked in the bamboo canes, stirred up the waves that fell against their little beach. Rain glistened on the great heart-shaped leaves of sea grapes, splashed off the eaves of the garage, dampened the east side of their silvery house to gray. And as Taylor stood in what had become a sunny mist, a double rainbow arched across the sky. She looked at it for a long time, then, holding her wet book bag tight, went into the house.

Grandmother Reddick sprang at her with a bath towel. "My goodness, child, I've been worried sick about you."

"Why?"

"Taylor, there has been a steady deluge for nearly an hour, and you out on your bicycle! I started to drive over and get you, but then despaired of finding you in such a storm—all those children at the school and I wouldn't know which entrance— Really, I've been beside myself."

Taylor, rubbing her head with the towel, said, "We have rains like this all the time, Grandmother."

"But you aren't always out on a bicycle, riding the highway, which must be dangerous enough under ordinary conditions, and what your father can be thinking of—"

"We're going to ride the bus from now on."

"Well, thank heaven for favors. Is that your *book* bag, Taylor? It's soaking, your books will be in terrible condition." She was getting Taylor's new schoolbooks out as she spoke. "I'll take care of these. Go up and change into something dry, dear. And then come down and tell me about school. Don't hang that wet dress in your closet, bring it down and we'll hang it in the laundry room."

"Where's Jem?"

"He telephoned and said he was visiting friends. The Dobkins?"

"Rod Dobkin," said Taylor, thinking, We do sort of limit ourselves. If it's the Howards, Grandmother is sure of the messsage. Any other name and she puts it as a question. "I'll go change. B.J.'s upstairs?"

"We've been playing Old Maid," said her grandmother, and Taylor nodded.

In the old days, B.J. would've been out splashing in the deep clean puddles created by the downpour. He'd have been sailing his toy boats in the runnels that rushed through sand and shells. He'd have been yelling at everybody to come see the rainbow. He'd have been outdoors, on such a day.

14

The fourth tropical storm of the season, named David by the United States Weather Service, was gathering strength near the Lesser Antilles in the Caribbean.

"I guess equal opportunity is giving men the right to have storms named after them," Jem commented. "It's about time."

"The other way around, dopus," said his sister. "Equal opportunity fixed it so that something as awful as a hurricane isn't always named after a woman. A really significant gain for the Cause, I don't think."

"What cause?"

Taylor studied him a moment and walked away.

The following morning, Tropical Storm David had become Hurricane David, with 155-mile-an-hour winds, and gales extending 150 miles out from its center.

"This could be bad," said Tony, and he took to looking at the barometer and listening to weather reports. Though there was no hurricane watch formally announced, residents of Florida started watching the track of David. Jem had a hurricane map pinned to his wall and was tracking the path of the storm with pins before he left for school in the morning and when he got back in the afternoon. Rains were now so heavy and unpredictable that he'd agreed to let his grandmother drive him to and from school. A couple of mornings during that first week of school, Grandmother even drove Taylor to the top of the drive and waited with her until the school bus came.

By Wednesday, David was said to be the strongest, the most vicious storm of the century. At school, boys who just happened to have the fateful name went about with chins and chests thrust out.

"Aren't they amazing?" Taylor said to Sandy at lunch.

"Who? Somebody's amazing?"

"Haven't you noticed that fellows named David are strutting around here as if the adjectives all applied to them? And as if they *liked* being called vicious and destructive? Not Mr. Gamble," she added. "Hey, you aren't listening."

"I'm worried about Amanda. I don't even seem to be able to concentrate on the storm. They say that hurricanes make depressed people more so. Do you think that's true?"

"Gee, I don't know. She's still refusing to go to school?"

"She says it's because of the cold sore. It's the worst cold sore I've ever seen. Even the old man agrees it's reasonable to stay home with a—a blemish like that. Except it's beginning to get better, so what happens then? It's how she's behaving, Taylor. Amanda's never frisked about like Pippa Passing, bringing joy to all beholders, but now she's so down it's—it's like living with a manic-depressive who's never manic. She's making me *very* jittery. It couldn't all be because of that mean scene in the john, except I think that was what finally smacked her down. Dr. Borden's ordered Librium for her. *He* says people who are depressed sometimes get more so in the hurricane season."

"He should know."

Dr. Borden was Amanda's psychiatrist. He was also Dan's, but Dan didn't speak to him. For a year, nearly, Dan had gone to Dr. Borden's office on Saturday mornings and sat for fifty minutes not saying a word. Everybody except Mr. and Mrs. Howard seemed to know about it, and it was odd.

"I suppose." Sandy poked at her fruit Jell-O. "If this

storm hits, there won't be any Labor Day party at our house. There may not be any house at our house. Or yours. I wonder where it will hit?"

"Maybe it'll miss Florida. It's awful to say that, isn't it? I mean, you keep hoping it won't come ashore where you are, a storm this bad, but it's going to slam down somewhere besides on those poor little Caribbean islands. Why should we wish it on somebody else?"

"Because we're human beings and human beings always want terrible things to happen to other people, that's why. Except for the cretins who think it'd be lots of exciting fun if it hit here. Amanda's hoping it'll wipe out all of Florida. She's got quite an ego, that girl. She'd eliminate an entire state just because she's in the dumps."

The bell rang and they left for the next class, which they had together in their homeroom with Mr. Gamble. If that doesn't cheer her up, nothing will, Taylor thought. Sandy loved math and had developed a crush on David Gamble. Not a big crush. Just enough to make her give up chocolate and perhaps take her mind off Amanda for a while. But as the hour went on, Taylor realized that so far as Sandy was concerned it might have been Big Foot at the front of the room explaining mathematical variables. Sandy's mind was not on Davids—Gambles or storms.

As the week went on, even Grandmother submitted to having her programs interrupted so that they could put on the weather station and listen to its ominous tidings. David, with winds still up to 150 miles an hour, hurled itself at Puerto Rico, Haiti, the Dominican Republic, weakened slightly over Cuba's mountain ranges, then set out for Miami. No one knew where it would go from there. Windows in public buildings, including their school, were webbed with masking tape. In the village shopping center, the market was emptied of candles, flashlights, batteries, its shelves all but swept bare of canned goods and bottled water. Merchants boarded their stores with plywood, and the police chief announced over the radio that evacuation centers had been set up around the county and that if an evacuation order came it would be carried out by force if necessary. In the past, the thing for swinging types to do had been to set up a hurricane party with lots of food and booze and then stay put. The Chief of Police said there would be none of that this time. People were to keep their transistor radios tuned for an announcement and were to go when he said go.

Tony ran *Loon* and the skiff into the bayou and tied them securely to a dock he'd built there ages ago. It had kept them safe in storms before. In a real hurricane—who knew? The canoe, B.J.'s little rowboat and the Sunfish were dragged up the beach, across the shell driveway to the edge of the woods. All the outdoor furniture, including the hammock, was carried into the garage, and about fifty hanging plants were transported to the woods and laid gently on the ground.

After that, Tony said, there was nothing further to

do except wait and see. "We'll take your car, Mother," he said. "Can't fit everybody and the dog and cat into the VW."

"The animals?" said Grandmother Reddick. "Can't we leave them at a veterinarian's?" She was thinking, Taylor knew, of animal hairs in her nice rented car.

"And suppose the vet got swept away?" Tony spoke kindly and frowned at Jem, who'd stiffened at the suggestion. His mother wasn't experienced about the ways of hurricanes, though she said they did have them in New England. "Tropical storms are different from those in the north," Tony said.

"Do you think we'll have to leave?" his mother asked, confident that Tony, her son, the Supreme Helmsman, would have the answer. He did not. He said it was still a long way off, and all they could do was wait.

Meanwhile the tides were four to five feet higher than usual, almost touching the bottom of their dock at high water. Surf on the Gulf side of the island could be heard booming day and night. On the bay side it hissed. And it rained. Torrentially, scantily, steadily, fragmentarily. The sun would blaze out from time to time, send mist curling over the water, rainbows curving over it, turn the woods into a fog-strewn dripping forest, and then desert the sky abruptly. Great flat mushrooms appeared that at night seemed to glow like ghosts at the edge of the trees, beside the house, in the grass that bordered the driveway.

And a new storm, Frederic, said at first to be a weak

tropical depression, all at once gained strength in the Caribbean where death and devastation, in the name of David, had mowed whole islands down.

On Friday Sandy asked Taylor to come home with her and spend the night.

"I'd like to," Taylor said. "But suppose the storm gets worse and we have to leave suddenly?"

"It's not that close," Sandy said sharply. "We have two or three days yet. But if you don't want to, okay."

"Ah, Sandy," Taylor said softly. "Of course I'll come. You're really worried about Amanda, aren't you?"

"I am and I'm not. Worried enough to be disagreeable to everybody, but not enough to call Dr. Borden yet. Which is what I keep thinking I should do."

"Hasn't she seen him this week?"

"She broke the appointment."

"What do your parents think?"

"Taylor! They don't think. They think she has a cold sore and is making a silly row about it. They think she's in a grot because of Alexander. I don't know what they think, except it isn't affecting their behavior in any way. That half-wit's still planning his stupid party. He thinks even hurricanes have to bend before his plans. He says the whole fuss is ridiculous, there hasn't been a storm of evacuating proportions for over ten years. That's supposed to reassure us and get the caterer to the house on time. And my mother's stoned every night and hung over every morning, so what's the point of talking to her?"

She didn't mention Dan. Taylor, who shared much of her life with her brothers, especially Jem, thought it was a pity, the way the three young Howards went their separate ways. Even if they didn't feel well and warmly welcomed in their parents' scheme of things, they could have had one another for comfort. Could have, but did not. At this stage of their lives, Taylor supposed, they wouldn't be able to change.

When she and Sandy got off the bus on Friday, the rain had let up. Taylor packed a few things in a canvas bag and told her grandmother where she was going. They walked through the village to Sandy's house, a place so large that when there was no human activity it seemed like some vastly empty stage set. Tony said it had taken a monster ego to build so pretentious a house, one so swollen with waste space and conspicuous consumption.

"You think of people on one side of the globe grateful for a cup of rice and a torn shirt," he'd said to Taylor once, "and then cast a glance at the Howards gorging themselves in every conceivable way. Not much need to wonder why anarchy is loose upon the world."

"Sandy says when she's eighteen she's going to leave home and never see her parents again or take anything from them as long as she lives."

"Be interesting to see if she feels that way in four years."

"Sandy always does what she says she's going to do," Taylor had said, and Tony looked skeptical.

Today as they came into the Howards' house, there was no sound except for the distant barking of Viva in Sandy's room. At present no one was working for the Howards, which was why they needed caterers for the Labor Day party. There was a cleaning service, but they only worked mornings. Dan was not to be seen. Mr. Howard, of course, was still at one or the other of his offices in one or the other of his banks. Mrs. Howard, the girls assumed, was in her room, but Sandy did not check to see. Amanda was certainly in hers. Sandy said that after they'd had a snack they'd try to coax her out for a visit. Amanda did not allow anyone in her room and she kept the door locked.

The kitchen, like the rest of the house, was big and clean and didn't look as if anything was ever used except the microwave oven. Sandy opened the door of a cavernous refrigerator, neatly stacked with labeled containers.

"Cheese and apples okay?" she asked. "O.J. or Coke?"

"Orange juice. Who's doing the cooking around here these days?"

"Nobody. We just shove something from the freezer into the Radarange. There's a new couple coming next week from somewhere in Virginia. I suppose when they read about these storms, they may opt out. I couldn't care less."

When they went upstairs and knocked on Amanda's door, there was no response. Sandy stood undecided for a moment, then said, "Why don't you go into my room? I'll look in on my mother and then see if I can get Amanda to come out."

"Okay."

Viva sprang about in a frenzy of greeting, and Taylor patted her absently. Usually she found this room beautiful, but today she wished she were back in her cozy tower. She walked to the window and stared down at the two swimming pools (one for adults, one for kiddies) set in their borders of imported tiles, surrounded by stretches of neat lawn. Here, too, mushrooms had appeared, blanched and spectral in the bright green grass. They were beautiful mushrooms, but Tony said not edible.

It began to rain again. Rain like billions of heavy gray strings falling straight down. The surfaces of the pools puckered and the entire prospect was such a downer that Taylor started to turn away. As she did, the corner of her expert eye caught a wing movement, and she stood hypnotized as a pileated woodpecker flew past the window and flattened himself against the trunk of a Sabal palm. He was huge, with a black back shining and wet as a beetle's. White neck stripes and a great scarlet crest. He was pressed against the tree, not drumming, not calling, just hanging there in the rain when Sandy came in.

"Come here," Taylor said, not turning. "Come look. On that palm over there."

"What *is* that?" Sandy asked.

"A pileated woodpecker."

"Looks like a survival from the Coal Age. Sort of creepy."

"He is not," Taylor said, but she laughed as they sat on cushions in the Japanesy "living" area of Sandy's big room. It was divided into three parts. "For sleeping, for studying, for living," said Sandy. "But it's dumb terminology. I expect the living is as lively, or as dull, in bedrooms or bathrooms or kitchens or whatever. Depend on who was doing it. I think it made more sense to call living rooms drawing rooms."

"Doesn't make sense unless you're an artist."

"Taylor. A drawing room was a room to which the ladies withdrew while the gentlemen had port and cigars and told gentlemanly off-color stories around the table. Golly, I'll bet men miss that sort of thing."

"Why didn't they call it a withdrawing room, then?"

"Parlor is a nice word," Sandy said. "Let's start calling our living rooms parlors."

"I think my grandmother does call hers a parlor. Did you talk to Amanda?"

"She won't come out. She's in there listening to Tom Waits celebrate the sediment of humankind. And she sounds *wired.* One touch and off she'll go, like Mariner Two."

"Where's Dan?"

"Amanda says he said he was going to the Dobkins' or to your house. He said he didn't want to stay here. Unaccountable, huh? But they weren't at your house. Jem or Dan, I mean."

"Did you ask your mother?"

"She's asleep. I'm going to call the Dobkins. I have to know if *any*one in my family is safe and sane." She dialed, spoke to Chrissie, hung up and said, "Both of them are there. Dan says he's going to stay all night because Daddy—he calls him *Daddy*—is at a Rotary dinner and won't notice he isn't home. Rotary night's usually good for an escape."

"What do you call him? I mean, when you're talking to him?"

"You. Out loud. Other things in the privacy of my own head."

"Isn't it funny how the Dobkins can always squeeze one more kid into that melee?"

"Phil Dobkin told me about one time when he had a friend visiting and at nine o'clock Mr. Dobkin said, 'Okay, everybody up to bed, scoot, no arguments.' And this kid was trying to explain he wasn't part of the family, just a visiting fireman, but Mr. Dobkin paid no attention—just herded everybody up to those sort of dormitories they have upstairs. Phil says the kid's parents had the cops out looking for him, but I don't know if that part is true. Maybe the whole story's apocryphal, but I tend to believe apocryphal stories, myself. Do you want to play Scrabble? Do you want to listen to my new album of *Grease*?"

"Let's do both."

By seven o'clock they were hungry. Amanda, invited through her closed door to come down and have a vegetable plate, declined shrilly. Mrs. Howard was still asleep. They descended to the kitchen and turned on a switch that lit the room like an auditorium. Sandy rooted in a large freezer for some foil-covered trays.

"What're we having?" Taylor asked.

"Let's see." Sandy consulted a typed list taped to the inside of the freezer lid. "Number six is chicken with the stuff that goes with chicken. Eleven is beef Wellington, etc. Five is scampi and so forth. What'll you have?"

"Scampi. Who does all this?"

"The last couple. The Martinezes. Handy, huh? They were pretty good cooks. We just pop the dishes in the Radarange. Instant gourmet dining. Why don't we take it up to my room on trays and eat Japanese style on my Japanese table?"

They tried once more to get Amanda to join them. This time she didn't answer at all.

"Well, I'm not going to think about her," Sandy said, as they put their dishes on the table and kneeled to eat. "Chopsticks okay?"

"Sure."

"It doesn't do any good, thinking about Amanda. People should be born without families, in my opinion."

"It's not a bad idea."

"Tell me about your granny. How's she taking the hurricane crisis?"

"She's leaving it up to Tony. He'll deal with it."

"Like King Canute, ordering the ocean to behave. Women that age are amazing. Even younger ones, like our mothers. Most of them bought the whole male package. It's hard to understand, considering the men they have to deal with. Now, Taylor—offhand and without thinking—tell me a man you think is really superior to all the women you know."

Taylor lifted her shoulders. "I can't. That doesn't mean there aren't any. It doesn't mean there aren't some women superior to men. I think I just don't know any superior types, except you. You're exceptional. I don't know *what* you'll do, but you'll make a mark of some kind one day."

"If there's a world left to make a mark in. I wonder about that a lot. I get to thinking about the future and what we'll do with it, and then get brooding about whether it'll be there by the time we get to it. The future, I mean."

"Sandy, if this were the last night of the world, right now, and you *knew* it, what would you do?"

Sandy thought for a long time. Then she said, "What I would want to do is take Viva and get out of this place. Go over to your house and spend the last night of the world in your tower room. Would we get to see the sunrise in your script?"

"Okay, we'll count in a sunrise. What do you mean, that's what you would *want* to do? It's the last night of the world—who's to stop you from doing what you want to?"

"Look—if it's really the last night of the world, I'd have to stay here with Amanda and my mother, wouldn't

I? I mean, neither one of them is really compos mentis and I can't just run out on them. Isn't that something? Even at the end of the world, a person isn't free to do what she wants."

15

At Taylor's house, before the arrival of Grandmother Reddick, somebody wanting to set the table for dinner had been apt to have to clear dishes left from lunch or even breakfast. But this evening, as soon as they'd finished eating, Sandy insisted on taking the supper things downstairs, where she rinsed the dishes and put them in the dishwasher.

"I don't see," Taylor said, watching, "why they're

called dirty dishes. They've only had clean food on them."

"They look dirty, after they've been eaten off of."

"Maybe."

"They attract cucarachas."

"You and Granny. You're a pair."

"I never said I didn't agree with some of her more reasonable notions. Let's go back and play some more Scrabble."

Taylor won a game, proving that Sandy's mind was not on it. Sandy had said once that it was better to live in a house divided than one that kept falling down on your head. Something like that. You don't get to choose, thought Taylor. That's the trouble. Nobody has any choice. But if I had to, or could, I'd take our house, even including Grandmother. There can't ever be any peace or security here. In the whole forty-eight hundred square feet of living space there can't be any certain knowledge of love or protection.

She wanted to reach out and pat her friend's hand. She wanted to say, "I understand, and I'll stand by. I'll always be here, when you need me."

But as it was, Sandy seemed to be just keeping her balance. Taylor had found that when she was floundering around trying to keep afloat and be brave, sympathy was apt to send the dam down and the waters tumbling after.

So she said nothing, but tried to beam subconscious messages of support as the next game progressed. She was working out what would have been a super seven-letter word, when Sandy's door was flung back to reveal Amanda, standing with her arms outspread.

"Sandy, I—want to tell you some—tell you something—"

She came into the room, swaying slightly, lurched to her knees, got up and climbed slowly onto a low sofa, where she sat weaving from side to side while Sandy and Taylor looked at her in growing fright.

What's the matter with her? Taylor wondered. What are we going to do with her? She glanced at Sandy, whose face had gone white under the honey tan.

". . . wantcha to know, li'l sister—want ver' ver' much you for you—for you t'know—" Amanda sighed, put her head in her hands, looked up and struggled on. ". . . I love you, Sandy . . . not sure if you ever knew it—but remem— remember that, will you—rem— 'member I did love—"

Sandy, shaken out of paralysis, was on her feet, shaking her sister's shoulders. "Amanda! Amanda, what have you been taking? You tell me what you've been taking!"

"Tha's for you to know . . . me to find out— Other way 'round, I supp— nothin' you can do, darlin' li'l sister—"

Sandy got down on her knees. "Please, please, Amanda—I beg you. Tell me what you've taken. What is it, was it? Please, Amanda! I can't stand this, I tell you . . . I cannot *stand* it!" Tears ran down her cheeks and she clasped her sister's hands in hers, shaking them roughly. "Amanda!" she shouted. "Answer me!"

"Shh," said her sister. ". . . you're so noisy, darlin'. . . . Think I'll go to sleep—"

"Amanda. You said you love me."

"Sure do, sure do, sure do . . . only one in whole shitty fam—"

"Then tell me what you've taken! I have to *know.*"

"Ah, honey . . . lessee—the Lib—"

"Librium. How much?"

"Oh, all . . . no point—halfway meas—"

"Anything else?"

"Lessee . . . aspirin—?"

"How much aspirin?"

"Hanful—six hanfuls—I'm goin' to sleep, honey . . . jus' wanted you to—" She sighed and tumbled sideways to the floor.

"Taylor, call the paramedics," Sandy said, leaning over her sister, pulling at her, trying to get her into a comfortable position.

"But—who do I dial? I mean, the operator?" Taylor asked shakily.

"There's an emergency number on the phone—oh god, it's on his private phone—down in his damn *den.* Go phone them. I'll use this one and phone—Dr. Borden. I'll call Dr. Borden. *Hurry,* will you?" She scrambled on her knees over to the telephone, her eyes on Amanda's prostrate figure.

Taylor flew down the stairs, along the hallway to the exceedingly dennish-looking room that was Mr. Howard's retreat, found the emergency number pasted on the telephone and dialed, her finger so shaky she had to hold it with the other hand. The paramedics were only a few blocks away, where they shared space with the volunteer fire department. The man who answered asked just one question and Taylor said, "I think—drugs."

"Right there," he said, and hung up.

Taylor took a deep breath and walked slowly into the hall, looked up the stairs, at the front door. She would not desert Sandy, but she was so frightened that she had to hold on to the banister as she went back up. Was Amanda going to die? Was she already dead? Taylor had never seen anyone dead.

"Is she— How is she?" she asked Sandy, who'd put a blanket over Amanda and was kneeling beside her, not touching her now.

"She's breathing."

In fact Amanda was breathing quite heavily, sort of snorting and snoring.

"Is Dr. Borden coming?"

"I couldn't get him."

"What about your regular doctor?"

"Couldn't get him either."

"Did you explain it was an emergency?"

"I told these very sympathetic recording machines that it was an emergency," Sandy said, and closed her eyes.

"The paramedics will be right here. I guess I forgot to open the front door."

"It's not locked. They'll come in." Sandy gave a sudden, frightening, loud cry, then clapped both hands over her mouth. She lowered them in a moment. "Sorry, Taylor. I—I've been thinking. When a person says—as Amanda has been known to say pretty often—that she can't stand being *inside* herself, that she wants to get out of her body, then somebody should have been paying a little more attention than we've been paying. If she dies, we're murderers."

"Oh, Sandy—"

"Including the great shrink, Borden. All of us. We just let her go on and on, dizzier and sicker and sadder every day, and nobody did a thing about it. Nobody."

"Sandy—"

Flashing across the ceiling, wavering in reflections of rain, came the lights of what Taylor hoped were the paramedics. She ran to the window. "They're here," she said. Two ambulances and a police car, with blue and red lights that fluttered in the darkness and the rain. People in yellow slickers, one carrying a rolled-up stretcher, one wheeling a tank. A person sees enough movies, she thought, to be able to guess that that's oxygen. She went out to the landing to direct them, but they seemed to flow up the stairs with no need of directions. She pointed toward Sandy's room anyway, then sat on the top step, chin in her hands.

A policeman, the one who'd brought B.J. home when he'd run away and who'd stopped Mr. Howard for speeding, mounted toward her. "How come you always show up?" she asked, then added, "That sounded rude. I'm sorry, Carl."

"Who is it?" Carl Orr jerked his head toward the room, from which came sounds of the paramedics at work. Through the open downstairs door, voices clamored over loudspeakers in the police car, in the ambulances.

"Why two?" she said. "Ambulances?"

"Who is it?" he repeated.

"Amanda."

"Mrs. Howard's in there with her? I'll have to talk with her," he said reluctantly.

Taylor closed her lips tight, and Carl started for the bedroom.

"Carl!" He turned, and Taylor said, "Don't. Not yet. I mean, Sandy's all alone with her sister, and it must be hard enough—not that they aren't wonderful—the medics, I mean. But there're so many of them," she said in confusion, her impressions scattering like grasshopper sparrows. "Her mother's not there, Carl. She's asleep. Not Amanda. Her mother. Except Amanda is, too."

They lived in a small village. Carl had grown up in it and Mr. and Mrs. Howard were among its more important citizens. Probably he, and everyone else, knew that Mrs. Howard was a "secret" drinker.

Carl cleared his throat. "Okay. Where's Mr. Howard?"

"At a Rotary dinner."

"I'll get hold of him. Tell one of the medics I want to see them, Taylor."

She tiptoed toward the door. Amanda was stretched

on the floor, an oxygen mask on her face. There were, after all, only three people on the rescue squad, and one was a woman. She came out of the room as Taylor approached it, nodded briefly and started downstairs. Taylor considered calling out that Carl wanted to talk to her, realized there was no need and went back to sit on the stairs again, leaning against the wall.

Voices mingled in the rain, and through the door she could see Carl and the young woman consult quickly before the medic went to call—whom? Someone to tell them what to do? Didn't they know what to do? They all looked pretty young. The woman came bounding back upstairs, past Taylor, into Sandy's room.

Taylor thought she should go in there with Sandy. She decided she'd be in the way if she did. She thought, Why does somebody do something like this? Why had Amanda done this thing? Life was scary, and sometimes awfully sad, and sometimes things happened that practically strangled a person with rage. But to take yourself out of it on purpose? To die? To *want* to die. She clasped her arms against her body, then jumped as the two men came out with Amanda between them on the stretcher. The woman wheeled the oxygen tank, holding the mask on Amanda's face.

As they went toward the stairs, the door to Mrs. Howard's room opened and she appeared, holding on to the door jamb, holding the folds of a fluffy blue robe together, holding—with some difficulty—her head up. She was flushed and puff faced, with disheveled hair. Her voice when she spoke was barely discernible. "What—what's happening?" she whimpered, and tottered toward the stretcher. She stood a moment, looking down at Amanda, then toppled softly to the rug.

The paramedics exchanged rather wild glances, then one of them said, "Emergency says to get her right over, *pronto,* and that's what we're going to do. Let's go. Carl can take over here."

Sandy looked at her mother a moment, then started after the stretcher.

"You can't come with us," the young woman holding the mask said, as they carefully maneuvered down the stairs.

"I'm not letting my sister go all alone to the hospital."

"She's not alone. There're three of us with her."

"I'm going, too."

"How old are you?"

"Sixteen," Sandy said quickly.

"I'll bet. Okay. But what about your mother? You just going to leave her there?"

"I've left her lying on floors before. Taylor," she called up the stairs. "Taylor, if she comes to—"

"Go ahead," Taylor said. "I'll stay till she—" But Sandy was already climbing into the ambulance beside her sister. They were gone, the two ambulances. Why two? Taylor wondered again, but never found out. They went slowly down the drive, lights flashing, sirens crooning, and disappeared in the rainy night.

Taylor looked down at Mrs. Howard. Should she just

leave her there, or try to shake her awake? Should she call her grandmother to come over and help? Grandmother Reddick didn't drink at all, but would not refuse to help someone who was—intemperate, she'd probably call it.

Carl came back in, closed the door behind him and ran up the stairs. "I got hold of Mr. Howard. He's going to meet them at the hospital. Let's help the missus back to bed."

He leaned down and picked up the fat little body with no seeming difficulty, looked around, then followed Taylor's glance to the right room. It was a lovely room with summer covers and draperies of glazed flowery chintz, an old four-poster bed with a tester, a beautiful rose-and-blue rug on parquet floorboards. There was even a fireplace. It had a pleated floral-printed fan in it. You'd think anybody who lived in such a pretty atmosphere would want to be conscious of it, Taylor thought, straightening the light dusty-rose covers, plumping the pillows. Her foot struck something and a bottle spun out from under the dust ruffle. Vodka and empty. She kicked it back out of sight. Carl, with no expression, put Mrs. Howard on the bed. Taylor drew the covers up, and they turned away.

"Taylor, they want me to look in Amanda's room and see if I can find any drugs besides Librium and aspirin."

"I'm sure there aren't any."

"You come with me."

"Amanda doesn't like people in her room. She never

lets *anyone* in it. Sandy says not even the cleaning crew. I don't think we should."

"Look, if she's taken something besides Librium and aspirin, the docs want to know."

"If we didn't find anything, they still couldn't be sure, could they? Anyway, aren't they the ones supposed to figure it out? Carl, is she going to be all right?"

"I think so. From what I heard Vera and the hospital doc saying to each other, if it's just aspirin and Librium in her system and she was conscious only"—he looked at his watch—"about fifteen minutes ago, she should be okay."

What's okay or all right for Amanda? Taylor wondered. Would she mean the same as we do when we say it? "What time is it?"

"Nine."

"Nine! I thought it was at least midnight."

Carl shook his head. "This's one of the toughest kind of calls. Almost worse than a car crash, in some ways. You and her sister—well, I'm sorry you've been put through this."

He doesn't, Taylor thought, seem to have much sympathy for Amanda. It seemed to her that for Amanda, when she came to—if she came to—*this*, as he called it, would just be starting.

"Let's get it over with," Carl said. "Will you open her door, please." He took his notebook out and Taylor, queasy and reluctant, tried the knob. Amanda had forgotten to lock up this time. Even in spring, during the house-and-garden tour, when the Howards' impressive residence was always on the list, Amanda's room was off limits and locked. Not now. Taylor pushed the door open, and they looked inside.

"Jeez," said Carl. "No wonder she don't want anyone in it."

The Reddicks, before Tony's mother had come to stay, had lived in disorder in a house far from clean, except for once in a while when Junie got a scouring streak and enlisted everybody's help. But they did not live in squalor, only in a mess. Here, in a house that Taylor had always thought of as *scraped* clean, was a room a pig would have had second thoughts about. The floor was strewn with crumpled clothing, records in and out of their jackets, magazines, dirty dishes. Really dirty dishes, some fringy with mold. The windowsills were jammed with pots of bean sprouts, alfalfa sprouts, jars of fruits and nuts and peanut butter from the Sprout Spout. Books toppled from shelves, clothes spilled out of drawers. In the closet most of the clothing was on the floor, and most of the room was in shadow. One bedside lamp with a torn shade illuminated a box of rusks, a half-eaten apple and a book of I Ching.

From the back of a chair to a window top and then over to a tall bedpost was a great spiderweb that Amanda had been protecting with an overlapping barricade of large cushions covered with dirty denim. Since no one else came in here, probably she'd been guarding against blundering into the web in the dark. Or maybe if she got high or something. Anyway, you could tell she was trying to preserve the web. In the precise center sat the creator of this huge construction, a black-and-white-and-red spider slightly larger than a ladybug.

Carl started to push the cushions aside with his foot but stopped when Taylor said quickly, "Don't do that!"

"Do what?"

"Move those. They're there to see that the spiderweb doesn't get broken. You can see that."

Carl rubbed his chin, studied the web, looked at Taylor. "Are you serious?"

"Yes. You can see the web's been there for a long time, and you can tell Amanda's been safeguarding it. We don't have a right just to break it down. She's an orb weaver, and it's really a super web."

"Who's an orb weaver? Amanda?"

"The spider."

"Everybody's crazy in this house. Why call it she? You can tell a female bug from this distance?"

"Most spiders that you see are female. The males get eaten pretty fast."

"Oh boy. By the females, of course."

"What else?"

He grinned and shook his head again. "Sometimes this job gets interesting, in a screwy way. Spiderwebs!" He looked around the room. "I can't search this place. How can anybody find anything? Let's try the bathroom." He stepped over clothes and magazines in his heavy shoes, opened the bathroom door, stood a moment wrinkling his nose. "Whew." The tub, the sink, the floor, were all grimy. Towels and sour-smelling washcloths drooped from the bars, fading posters of fading rock stars clung to the walls. The Librium bottle was in the sink, empty. Aspirin tablets were broadcast like big white seeds. Taylor's stomach turned as she saw grayish fungus growing out of cracks between the tub and the wall.

She backed away, Carl following.

"There's no way to search for anything in this garbage dump," Carl grumbled. "I'll have to see what the Chief says. Let's get out before we catch typhoid."

In the hall they looked at each other cautiously. Carl, after all, was pretty young still, and he'd grown up in the habit of respecting the Howard family because of all that money, all those banks. He was shocked, and it showed, by the whole night's business. Amanda, Mrs. Howard, that *room*—

"Do you have to tell?" Taylor asked hesitantly.

"About what?"

"Well—" She gestured toward Amanda's room, glanced at Mrs. Howard's closed door. "About any of it?"

"Of course I do," he said sharply. "I went out on a call, and I gotta report on it. All of it."

"I see."

"Maybe you see or maybe you don't. But I've got a job to do."

"I see," she said again. After a moment, she added, "What now?"

"Damned if I know." He looked toward Mrs. Howard's room. "We can't just leave her here alone. But I'm not going to leave a kid here alone with her, either. And I have to call in. I'll call in and see what the Chief says."

He went back down to his car, to talk to his chief, returned and this time trudged up the stairs. Taylor was sure he wasn't tired. He probably wouldn't get tired at ten times this much work. He was disgusted. That was what was slowing him up.

"They're sending a policewoman to sit with—" He jerked his head toward Mrs. Howard's door. Banks and money would never restore Carl Orr's respect for the Howards.

"I wish you hadn't done that," she said. "It's all going to be—such a disgrace."

"It all *is* a disgrace."

Maybe in order to be a policeman, she thought, you had to be hard this way, had to not care about people's feelings. She remembered the time Carl had driven B.J. and Drum back from that naked excursion. He'd been very kind that day, and concerned. So, this was how the Chief of Police had told him to handle it and he didn't have any choice, and there wasn't a chance that the doings of tonight would remain unknown.

They waited until the policewoman arrived and then Carl drove Taylor home.

Grandmother Reddick and Jem were looking at a movie and they turned when she came in.

"I thought you were spending the night with Sandy," Grandmother said.

Taylor pulled at a strand of hair. "Amanda's sick. She had to go to the hospital."

"Oh, dear. How sudden. Is she bad?"

"They don't— The paramedics, they came for her—apparently they think she's going to be all right."

"But what's the matter with her?"

"I don't know," said Taylor, and that was certainly the truth.

16

On Saturday, Taylor waited uneasily to hear from Sandy. She didn't want to call the house, for fear of getting Mrs. Howard. Or mister. She felt sure Amanda hadn't died. Sandy would have let her know if that had happened. Amanda, she thought, probably never had intended really to die. She'd taken some pills to scare people into understanding that she needed someone to care about how desperate she was feeling. Somebody to pay attention to her and know how to help her. Well, she'd kicked up a tremendous row and brought all kinds of people into it and word would be all over the village about what she'd done. How was Amanda going to face people now? If you kill yourself, at least you don't have to look anyone in the eye afterward and try to—to keep your dignity. If you try to kill yourself (even if you aren't really trying) and don't bring it off, you'll surely be faced with scornful, furtive, curious, even compassionate glances from all eyes. And even compassionate ones, Taylor thought, would be hard to take.

How was Amanda going to manage, after this, when things had been so bad for her before?

Sitting alone on the outside front porch, with the sun glittering on the bay, its restless waters the only sign that havoc was crying across the Caribbean, she thought about Amanda, maybe trying to kill herself, and about those people down there on devastated islands, trying to survive. Not to save a thing except their lives, because the storm was too powerful for any effort except that. But those little islands, Martinique and Dominica, were poor, and now the people who had lived through the hurricane would have nothing, and they'd had little enough before. This morning, by radio, Premier James Oliver Seraphine had told the world in a distant, exhausted voice, "Dominica does not exist anymore." It was awesome, and awful. But why was it so difficult to feel the afflictions of faraway people? Something terrible was happening to those human beings, but in Florida everyone was just hoping that David, when he hit the mainland, would hit somewhere else. Here she could sit and feel, really feel, just dreadful for Amanda, but only screw up her face in an effort to comprehend that four hundred people who'd huddled in a church for safety had been swept away by a torrent and drowned. Four hundred people. And an entire island destroyed. Their homes and farms and shops and churches gone. Nowhere for them to be dry, or fed, nowhere for them to feel safe. And Frederic, growing stronger, roaring toward them, while she sat here worrying about a girl she knew who was unhappy. Was she worried about Amanda, or for Sandy?

Either way, she wished she'd hear.

On the porch railing a green lizard did push-ups and inflated the pink petal beneath his chin. A darling gesture, though a threatening one. Taylor looked around to see who was menacing his turf, saw nothing, went on watching this minute survivor of the age of dragons. If you tried to grab a lizard, he could usually get away by leaving his tail thrashing in your fingers. Off he'd scuttle, to grow a new tail in time, and you'd be left holding the writhing remnant of his old one. Metaphorically thinking, and it was a way Taylor liked to think, you could say that Junie in her desperation to escape had slipped away leaving her old life wriggling in their hands. No doubt Junie would grow a new tail, a new life. After a moment—or whatever time it took for you to realize you were left with a moribund scrap of something that had got away from you—you threw the scrap away, tossed the tail into the bay. You didn't go on thinking about it.

Not to make a metaphor of it, it appeared that they were getting accustomed to not seeing Junie's face. As she thought this, Taylor felt a surge of tears.

Why the heck didn't Sandy call? She got up and went to the downstairs telephone, picked it up and heard her mother's voice.

". . . and I don't mean to be an alarmist, Tony, but will you get the *hell* off that island?"

"When I think it's necessary, we'll get off," said her father.

Taylor held the receiver tight against her ear. People could usually tell when someone had picked up the extension, but probably they were too absorbed in what they were saying to notice.

When she'd first left, Junie had written each of them a letter. Tony had read his aloud to them. Taylor didn't know what Jem had done with his or if he'd answered it, but hers was still unopened in a drawer in her room. This was the first time her mother had telephoned. *Was* it the first time? She and Tony didn't sound as if they hadn't spoken to each other in weeks.

"Now see here, Tony," her mother went on, "you have my kids down there with you, and I have a right to demand that you get them off that island!"

"Your kids?"

A silence, and then Junie said, "Yes. My children. I

don't care how much you can't understand how much you are responsible for the mess we're in, but those are, always have been, always will be, my children as well as yours. Make no mistake about that."

"Okay. So I won't make a mistake about that."

"Tony—have you ever, ever once, asked yourself why I did this? Have you spent all your time feeling aggrieved and sorry for yourself and not even a moment trying to figure out why it happened?"

Tony hung up. There was a silence, and then Junie, who apparently *had* heard the extension picked up, said softly, "Taylor? Is that you?"

Taylor held the receiver briefly against her breast, cradled it softly and went up to her tower room and cried for a long time. It was almost delicious, to cry at such length, but the time came when she sat up dizzily, blew her nose, wiped her eyes, stared out of the window that faced the Gulf. A big sailboat was galloping over the gusty seas. Crazy, she thought. Crazy people, to go out on a day like this.

She got up and went to her bureau, reached under some blouses and brought out the letter from Junie. Postmarked five weeks ago. Sitting on the bed, she turned it around in her hands, then carefully opened the envelope, drew out the single sheet of paper, looked out the window again for a long time before glancing down at her mother's big scrawly handwriting.

"Taylor dear, this will not be long, and if I know you, it may not be read, but I want to say that useless thing that people always say in hurtful situations. I love you. I love you very very much and nothing I do will ever change that. No way you react to what I've done will change it, either. I could hope that one day you'd understand—without my having to outline failings on my part and your father's—what made me feel I'd choke if I didn't get away. You could try to understand, without outlines. Do that for me, if you feel like doing something for me. Love, Junie."

Taylor put the letter back in the envelope, back in the drawer, and tried to cry again but could not, so she decided to go over to the beach and walk. Too rough to go in the water today. Crazy people in sailboats might go out from safe harbor, but she would just walk in the wind and watch the shorebirds and wonder, as she always did in fierce storms, how they found protection for themselves from rain and gales. Was it part of nature's plan that no bird should be nesting during the hurricane season, no eggs hatching, that fledglings should all be fledged? She'd walk beside the ocean and think about birds, and about herself and her mother and poor Amanda—

The phone rang.

"Taylor? Taylor, will you do me a great huge favor?"

"Sure, Sandy."

Sandy gave a laugh that was half sob. "Who wouldn't love you? No *Well that depends.* No *Tell me first what it is.* Just *Sure.*" She stopped.

"Okay, what're we going to do?" Taylor asked. But

she already knew and listened dispiritedly to Sandy's explanation.

"My parents are too furious or too hung over—sort that out for yourself—to go to the hospital. But Taylor—somebody has to go see her. We can't just leave her there by herself, *thinking.* I can't stand to think what she can be thinking. And I can't—I mean I don't want—to go alone. I'm—sort of scared. The bus to town goes by in fifteen minutes. Would you meet me there?"

"Okay."

She ran upstairs, changed her shorts for a skirt and blouse, stopped to tell her grandmother, but not her father, where she was going and ran to the bus stop.

On the way to town they talked about hurricanes. The females of the species were not so deadly. Elena was whirling weakly around in the Gulf of Mexico, and Gloria was twisting her way over the Atlantic. It was David and Frederic that had Florida frightened.

"Tony says we've got everything lashed down and stowed away as well as we can, and we've each got a bag packed in case we have to run for it. But he says we'll wait until the order comes to leave."

"We're going to Dayton. There's some kind of bankers' meeting there, so he can escape and do business at the same time. He says by the time the order comes to evacuate, there'll be such a crush to get out that the traffic jams will be miles long. Maybe he's right, Taylor. I mean, two bridges between us and the mainland and both of them two-lane. Maybe you should leave."

Taylor thought of Junie's call. *Will you get the* hell *off that island?* But here they still were, and would be until Tony decided otherwise.

"He's already running the hurricane blinds down," Sandy went on. "You people should get those. They're safe for winds up to a hundred fifty miles an hour."

"Tony says we can't afford them."

"Can you afford to have your house inundated?"

"I don't care."

"Of course you do, Taylor. You love your house. I love it, too. It's so—"

"Scrunchy," Taylor suggested.

"That's just what it is. Scrunchy." There was silence and then Sandy said, "I understand you and that policeman saw her room." Taylor nodded. "My parents went in there today and cracked, absolutely cracked. He's out of his tree. He's like a berserk gorilla. And she's spent the morning throwing up. I felt like puking myself. How did she manage to *get* it in that condition? It would take *work* to do that."

"No," said Taylor, more of an expert at slob living than Sandy. "No, you just never pick up, never wash anything, and in no time you have a properly filthy accumulation." She shuddered, remembering the fungus in Amanda's bathroom, but couldn't speak of it. "What I can't understand is how she contrives to look so fresh and clean *herself,* when she's coming out of that pigpen every day."

"I noticed she'd been using the guest bathroom for

showers and all she ever wears is jeans and tee shirts. I suppose she just tosses them in with other people's wash. I don't know. It's sick, that room. My mother's going to have it fumigated and scrubbed down, and he says there's going to be morning inspection, like at West Point." She leaned her head back, closed her eyes briefly. "How is she going to stand it, Taylor? And how are they going to face her? They're both so ashamed, so *mortified,* that they can't get around to what they should be doing—worrying. I mean, he's worrying his teeny head off about what people will think of him, and he's also worried to death about the hurricanes, but all he's doing about Amanda is planning suitable punishments."

Taylor didn't know what to say.

They got off in front of the hospital, inquired about Amanda at the information desk and were directed by a volunteer in pink to a wing on the third floor. "The psychiatric wing," said the volunteer, brightly important behind her desk.

Sandy glared at her. "Could you repeat that in a louder voice? I don't think everyone in the hospital managed to hear you." She spun on her heels. "Come on, Taylor, let's go—"

Sandy, usually so calm and composed, was beginning to split at the seams.

Amanda had a private room. An airy, flowery, at the moment sunny private room. With bars on the windows. She was sitting up in bed, looking—despite the cold sore—pretty, perky, quite at ease.

Sandy and Taylor stood gaping in the doorway.

"Darlings!" Amanda cried out. "Come in, come in! Did you bring me some nighties, Sandy? I don't want to be in this so-called gown that looks like a sailbag any longer than I have to. Let me introduce you to my dragon in the chair over there."

A large solid woman in a nurse's uniform sat in an armchair in a corner. Unsmiling, unfrowning, she glanced at the two girls, looked away.

"She's here to see I don't jump out the windows," Amanda said in a fluting tone. "Note the bars, please. Still, that's what she's here for. To see that I don't get away somehow. She speaks not, neither does she spin. Neither does she read or have any pulse. I'm not sure she hears or thinks—anyway, there's been no indication of activity in that direction. She is here because I am finally and officially a nut case—which is sort of a relief, you know—and Ophelias must be kept an eye on, or the first thing you know out the window and down the river they go, right? I *tried* to get out of bed once, just to go to the bathroom, and she *hurled* me back in and *produced* a bedpan, and said they'd put restraints on me if I tried such a *madcap* trick again. That's my 'madcap,' not hers. Restraints is subtle for straitjacket. Do you suppose she could really do that? Do you suppose I could wear a nighty over a straitjacket?"

"Amanda," Sandy said, "stop it. Don't."

"Don't what, honey? Don't talk, don't breathe, don't think, don't take pills? Don't what?"

Sandy said to the woman in the chair, "Can you leave us for a while?" The woman shook her head. "Look, *we're* here. I'm her sister and this is her friend and we aren't going to help her pull the bars out—"

"No," said the woman.

"Wait here," Sandy said to Taylor and went out of the room. In a few minutes she was back with a nurse. This one looked like a real nurse. Taylor wasn't sure what the difference was between her and the woman in the chair, but a difference was there.

"Mrs. Prothero," said the nurse, "you may sit in a chair out in the hall while Miss Howard sees her visitors."

The woman got up and marched to the hall. Oh boy, Taylor thought. That weirdo is supposed to look *after* weirdos?

"I'm Ms. Mears, charge nurse on this floor," said the nurse. "When will your parents be in?" she asked Sandy.

"I'm not sure," Sandy said grimly. "But they'll be here."

"Oh, not on my account, please," Amanda protested. "Anyway, I expect they'll come only if I indicate repentance." She lowered her voice, trying to imitate her father's. "I can forgive a Magdalen, but I want her to be repentant." She smiled. "Not that I'm really a Magdalen, mind. One Alexander does not a strumpet make. See if you can keep them away from me, Sandy."

"Now, Miss Howard," said the nurse. "You don't mean that."

"Now Ms. Mears, I most definitely do. Why do you suppose I'm in this cuckoo's nest to begin with? *You'd* be here, if you had my parents."

"Is that a way to talk about your own people?" Ms. Mears said automatically.

"I can think of other ways," said Amanda.

Ms. Mears sighed, looked at the two girls. "Not a long visit. Miss Howard needs rest."

"That's certainly what I need. Rest. And you know what they give me to get it? Pills. There's irony for you, Sandy." When Ms. Mears had gone, Amanda's voice dropped a bit. "*Don't* look so woebegone, Sandy. I'm all right."

"All right? Okay, so you're all right. Anyway, you're safe here, if David hits."

"Thank you for calling my attention to that. I'll be safe and you'll be drowned."

"Probably not. We're going to evacuate early, he says. We're going to Dayton. Some board of directors' meeting."

"The meeting of the board of brigands will please come to order in Dayton. Isn't evacuate the foulest word? Wouldn't you think they could think of something else? Couldn't they say run away, flee, escape—*anything* except evacuate. Must be the official mind. Scatological. I see you have your tote bag, Sandy, and I *hope* you have some books for me. I didn't have time to grab a few on my way out last night."

Is this bravado? Taylor wondered. Or is she really

out of touch with things? How would they go about finding out? Would it be Dr. Borden making the attempt, or would he be fired for not picking up signals? Could psychiatrists always pick up signals? Dan, for instance, never saying one word to the man for a year. How could he get a signal from that? Or was that the signal?

"Taylor, your dear face is all twisted up," said Amanda. "What are you thinking? Oh no, don't tell. Sandy doesn't think people should ask people what they're thinking, although personally I sometimes really want to know and how can I find out if I don't ask, unless I'm dealing with a very forth*coming* person, like Alexander, who talked about what he was thinking all the time—and guess what it was? His identity. Alexander thought about his identity constantly. He assumes he has one, but I'm not absolutely sure of that. What books did you bring me, Sandy?"

"My Family and Other Animals. Come Hither. The House of the Seven Gables."

"Oh good. Everything to reread, nothing new to face. You always know just what to do, Sandy."

"Just what are you going to do?" Sandy burst out.

"About what? When?"

"About everything. Ever. What do you *want,* Amanda?"

"Well, I want my spiderweb to be there when I go back, if I have to go back, but I know there isn't a chance of that and I mustn't waste wishes. I do get three, don't I?"

"I wasn't giving you wishes, Amanda. I'm not empowered to hand those out. I only wondered . . ." Sandy's voice trailed off sadly.

"You wondered what I want. I want never to go back to that house, or to see those two people again. But there's no chance of that either. There, I've used up all three wishes, just like in the fairy tales. Funny that nobody can ever make those wishes work out right—when I used to read those stories I always thought how *dumb* the people were not to think before they spoke. I always thought how much better I'd manage, if I got a chance. . . ."

17

The Howards went to Dayton, Ohio, and David went to Palm Beach and Cape Canaveral. Labor Day passed unobserved because of heavy rains, and school reopened on schedule the day after. Frederic continued as a capricious menace in the Caribbean, gaining and losing strength and form. Some of the village merchants took the plywood down from their windows, and others just stayed on vacation, uncertain of Frederic's potential, unwilling to deboard and then board again in what was, after all, the off-season still. The temperature stayed in the nineties by day and barely dipped into the eighties at night, and Grandmother Reddick suffered. She carried paper towels with her, to blot her perspiring face and neck, and continued to cook roasts for the evening meal. But most of her time was spent in her room, even though that meant black and white instead of color. Most of B.J.'s time, therefore, was spent in there, too. Drum, not allowed in, lay disconsolately in the hallway. Tut was usually out now, except at night when he slept with Jem. The pastry chef's back was acting up again, which meant that Tony was almost never at home.

"Gee," said Jem. "Gosh."

"I know," said Taylor.

"Do you suppose we'll ever get used to it?"

"I guess so. I mean—what else?"

"I'd like to see a walking catfish."

"So would I."

"I read about this lady kept one in her aquarium and every time it rained the catfish jumped out and walked around the living room. She had to get rid of it. It scared people."

"Why jump out because it's raining? They're already in water."

"For some unplumbable reason they like to walk in the rain. Apparently this catfish wanted to be let out of the door."

"Can't blame him for that," said Taylor, who loved

to walk in the rain. "How do they do it? Walk?"

"Lock their pectorals into position. Sort of like a person propelling himself on his elbows. Sea cows could do it, too, I bet, except they're so big. You know, you read where human beings originated from these little things that took a chance and came out of the water to live on land. Maybe the walking catfish are going to develop into something else. Turn into another species."

"If they do, I hope it isn't humanoid. One species like ours is enough to finish off the planet."

"But think if a whole lot of catfish walked out of the bay right now and came into the house."

"I don't think I'd like it."

"Me either, but it'd sure be some sight."

On Friday the Howards returned, rolled up their hurricane blinds and went to visit Amanda. Sandy, coming over to see Taylor in the evening, looked wan.

"I'll make a snack for us," Taylor said, "and we can eat it out on the porch."

"Thanks, Taylor. I don't want anything."

"Not even Tony's apricot-pistachio bars?"

"No. But thanks."

"Well, let's sit out there and look at the storm."

They slumped on the swing and watched as clouds that look gray and solid as iron massed on the horizon, illuminated from behind with an electrical display like strobe lights. Thunder rumbled distantly, but directly overhead were stars, and no rain fell.

"You know," said Sandy, "I was reading the other day that the Supreme Court says a child—that's a minor, like us, or Amanda—can be committed by parents to a mental institution and the kid doesn't have any right to a lawyer or a hearing or anything. One shrink, a lawyer and a parent—and there you are in the butterfly net. And the things they can railroad you *for*, you wouldn't believe. Foul language. Misbehavior. What in hell is misbehavior?"

"It seems to cover a lot of ground. Is that actually what the Supreme Court said?"

"That's what the newspaper said it said, and I suppose they wouldn't misquote. A psychiatrist and the parents can determine what exactly, in the case at hand, is misbehavior. It's scary, having the Supreme Court against you."

They were silent for a while, and then Taylor said, "What did you do in Dayton?"

"You can't do anything in Dayton. We stayed in a hotel and he went to the board of brigands' meeting—I like that, don't you? I almost refused to go to Ohio with them, I thought I'd stay here with you, but then I read about the Supreme Court decision and how do I know he hasn't read it too? I was afraid to kick up too much of a row. My god, we're helpless—you realize that, Taylor? Absolutely helpless. Amanda and Dan and I not only have him to contend with, now we've got the nation's highest tribunal."

"Is he going to put Amanda in an institution?"

"Seems as if. Actually, she doesn't mind. Actually, she's looking forward to it. The way Dr. Borden describes it—"

"They're still using him?" Taylor interrupted.

"Would you believe it? Somehow he snowed them. Amanda wasn't forthcoming, she kept things from him, so how could he guess and so on and so on. They bought it. I thought the shrinks were supposed to root around and uncover the stuff that was being kept from them. I thought that was their job. Anyway, Dan's quit. He finally told the old man he hadn't been saying anything for a year and didn't plan on saying anything next year and Dr. Borden told them that Dan's therapy is completed, and that much has been accomplished by silence. I don't know. Maybe much has. At least Dan had the nerve to quit. So how do we know it wasn't something Dr. Borden did that made him able to quit?" Taylor had never known Sandy to sound so hesitant, so unsure of herself. "Anyway, there we are."

"But where's Amanda?"

"Tomorrow they're taking her to this country-club-sounding banana box outside of Tampa. Dr. Borden says let's transfer her before there's any more trouble with Frederic, and then—she stays there."

"Till when?"

Sandy shrugged. "Till they decide she leaves. After that, she's going to a boarding school up north, in Virginia. The idea seems to be to remove her from the family situation, which I personally think is the neatest idea Dr. Borden ever had. I'd like to be removed from my family situation. Boy, how I'd like it."

"Will you miss her?"

"Ah, Taylor. Not really. You know that. She's too weird for me, and after that punch-up the other night she scares me. No, I want what's best for her, but I don't mind if what's best lies someplace where I am not." She sighed. "How I wish I were eighteen. I'd do anything but die to be eighteen."

"Junie telephoned the other night."

Sandy swung around to face Taylor. "You know, I should be put in the public stocks. All I have done for—for ages—is talk about myself—"

"Not about yourself. About your family."

"Certainly not about you. Have I even noticed how you're feeling? I have not. How are you feeling? How is Grandmother Reddick?"

"She's suffering from the heat. She has some kind of temperature regulator that's different from everybody else's. We're all hot, but she's percolating. And I'm okay."

"What did Junie *say* to you?"

"She wasn't talking to me. She phoned Tony to tell him to get us off the island because of David. I just listened in." She let out an uneven breath. "Tony hung up on her, but she knew I was on the line, or she knew someone was and guessed me, because she said, 'Taylor, is that you?' "

"And?" Sandy asked gently.

"I hung up on her, too."

They sat for a long time watching the striations of dark and light, coppery and silver streaks that wavered in the sky.

"It must be like the aurora borealis," Sandy said.

A great blue heron—Benjamin? Taylor wondered. Beatrice?—landed on the dock and drew up one leg, settled the long neck on its shoulders and prepared to rest. They could hear mullet jumping in the dark, and under the dock the sliding, sucking waters of an incoming tide.

"You want to spend the night?" Taylor asked. "I've got a jigsaw puzzle started. All grass and sky. Very hard."

"That'd be fine. I'll phone and tell them. Dan's gone to the Dobkins' again. I guess staying out of the family atmosphere is getting to be second nature with us. Where's Jem?"

"At the Dobkins'. Do you suppose there's another happy family in the world, besides the Dobkins? They just go on and on being happy and nice and welcoming and warm. Are there any others like them, do you think?"

"I'd imagine there'd have to be. We just haven't run across another such in fourteen years. I think I'll take one or two of those apricot-pistachio bars now."

Tropical Storm Frederic regained strength as it moved across Cuba. Forecasters said it might again be upgraded to a hurricane once it got over water. Small craft in the Florida keys and southeast Florida were warned to exercise caution. Out in the Atlantic, east of the Azores, Hurricane Gloria whirled wrathfully along shipping lanes. Elena disappeared. Hurricane David, once feared and vicious, swept New England with wind and rains and vanished in icy North Atlantic waters.

By Monday evening, Frederic was definitely a hurricane, entitled to all the adjectives of his precursor. Again Floridians were told to take precautionary measures. At school the gymnasium was declared out of use for athletics so that cots, blankets, water jugs and food supplies could be stored there. In the event. There were certain words and phrases you heard now over and over. In the event. Evacuation. Emergency preparedness. Small craft stay close to port. And, by Tuesday, from Cape Sable to Tarpon Springs, from Tarpon Springs to Apalachicola, small craft should remain in safe harbor.

Frederic, a monster copycat, was following the path of his giant predecessor, and both coasts of Florida were again alerted.

"Why can't they tell which way it's going?" Grandmother Reddick asked Taylor when she came in from school on Tuesday afternoon.

"They predict a lot better than they used to," Taylor said, dropping her books on the dining-room table, picking them up again at a glance from her grandmother. All the surfaces in their house, from floor to ceiling, were now so spotless and gleaming that it was difficult to know where to put anything.

"This is so unsettling," Grandmother Reddick said. "One storm after another. Is it always like this?"

"Hasn't been for years. Besides, the hurricane season is almost over. If we can get to October without being hit, we'll be pretty safe. Except there've been hurricanes as late as November, sometimes."

"Very reassuring. Oh, you had a letter from your mother this morning."

Taylor caught her breath, felt her heart begin to thud. "Where is it?" she asked nervously.

"Over there on the desk. She doesn't say much, but I must say, Taylor, it's odd of you to listen in on telephone calls and even stranger to hang up on your own mother, no matter what she's done."

A gust of anger struck Taylor dumb. She stood staring at her grandmother, her mouth dry, her body trembling with rage. Unable to bring herself to speak, she turned and started for the stairs.

"Aren't you going to read your letter?" Grandmother Reddick called after her.

Taylor turned, ran her tongue across her lips, took a deep breath to steady her voice and said, "Why should I, since you already have?" Ignoring her grandmother's indignant demand that she explain herself, she went up to her room, pushed a chair under the doorknob, then sat on the bed with tightened mouth and narrowed eyes, staring out the window.

When, presently, the knob turned and the door was pushed in vain, she continued to stare straight ahead, and when the knock came, and the demand that she come out of there immediately, how did she dare barricade herself in this fashion, she continued to look out the window.

Later, when Jem knocked and said wasn't she coming down for dinner, she called out shortly, "No, I'm not, and don't ask me again."

"Suit yourself. What's Grandmother in such a swivet about?"

Taylor didn't reply.

Shortly after midnight came Tony's knock. "Taylor, may I come in?" he asked.

She moved stiffly, having been lying motionless on her bed for hours, one arm over her eyes. She took the chair away and opened the door. "I have to go to the bathroom," she said. "Be right back."

Tony was sitting in the armchair when she returned. He looked desperately tired, but Taylor refused to be touched by that. "Well?" she said.

Tony rubbed his eyes, coughed, looked across at her where she sat on the bed. He looked as if he didn't know how to begin and would have welcomed help, but Taylor gave him none. After a while he said, "Junie and I never pried into your lives. We don't believe in it." He waited. Taylor waited. "Okay," he resumed. "It's shocking to you that somebody should open and read a letter addressed to you. But my mother's of a different generation—"

"Would she open your letter?"

"No, but—"

"But you're an adult and she wouldn't dare. I'm a child. She has no more respect for children than the Supreme Court does."

"The Supreme Court?"

"Skip it."

"Taylor, you're going to have to apologize to her for how you acted this afternoon. She's dreadfully upset."

"You're kidding, aren't you?"

"I certainly am not. She's more upset than I've seen—"

"Tony! I meant, you're kidding that I have to apologize to her. You have to be."

"Well, I'm not, and you're going to. If this house is going to function at all we have to have some standards of courtesy."

"You mean I have to apologize to her because she opened my mail?"

Tony's hands flew to his forehead. He looked like someone trying to hold his head on and when he spoke his voice was gritty. "Taylor—are you trying to make my life more wretched than it already is? You don't even try to get along with her. I can feel your rancor and resentment, all the time. It's poisoning our lives. There's no damned peace in my life anywhere, and you should be trying to help me. Who've I got, besides you and Jem, to give me a little—a little—" He looked up and said, "Okay. I'm wrong in what I ask. I know it. This whole situation is just as hard on you as it is on me, and I have no right to ask more than—than whatever you feel you can give. And of course she should not have opened your mail. I didn't think I'd have to tell you I knew that. I thought you'd know I knew it. I was asking you to be—generous."

This must be what he does with Junie, she thought. First he asks something impossible, then says he knows it's impossible and he has no right to ask, and all the time he's looking at you with these sad betrayed blue eyes, making you feel guilty because your rights have been trampled on.

"I'll apologize to her," she said.

Tony nodded. "It's just—in a situation like this, Taylor, there's no reaching her. I can reach you. But my mother never has been able to see that there are two sides to every question."

"There aren't two sides to this question. I'll apologize because you want me to, but she's wrong and doesn't have a side."

She was hoping he would say, "Don't do it, Taylor. Don't go against your conscience just to keep the peace." He didn't. He got up, walked to the door, turned and said, "I appreciate it, Taylor. Thank you." He sounded extremely tired.

"Good night, Tony," she said.

The pastry chef returned to work again and told Tony to take a night off, so Friday evening found him lying on the sofa, hands beneath his head. He seemed to have his eyes fixed on a picture of Notre Dame in the snow that had replaced Junie's intaglio of the fish that killed each other. Jem had the TV on, turned to the weather station, but was not listening. He'd gone through all the books Sandy had left for him. Now he was reading *The Master of the Ballantrae* and planned to read all through Robert Louis Stevenson. B.J. was in bed, Grandmother Reddick up in her room. Taylor had spread a cloth on the dining-room table to do her homework there.

In the night the wind lashed treetops and shrubbery, sighed down the chimney, stirred through the room. Rain drummed on the tin roof over the outside porch and streamed down black windows.

The elements raged in the dark, but once again they'd got off easily here on their part of the coastline of Florida. Hurricane Frederic had charged past them into Alabama, crippling the city of Mobile, wrecking beachfront communities. Houses, trees, whole islands. Once again, on earlier TV reports, there had been those pictures of people wandering through the remnants of their homes, picking up a pot here, a toy there, then turning to face the camera and say, "Well, we'll just have to rebuild. What else can we do?" Birds, when their nests were blown down by gales, sometimes rebuilt, but often just took wing and removed themselves from the situation. People couldn't do that. They had to stay, try to salvage what they could and then rebuild.

We're all safe here, Taylor thought. Our house is

whole, we aren't hungry. Even the animals had had sense enough to come in from the storm. Tut lay over there on Jem's lap, Drum was dreaming on the floor beside B.J.'s bed. But you couldn't help wondering, from the lamplit center of your security, what those people in the Caribbean, in Alabama, were doing at this moment, living without walls or roofs or light to see by. Some without food. You couldn't help wondering what sort of world it was where there was plenty of food but thousands and thousands of people were starving to death and no government could get food to them. What was the matter with human beings, that they were able to starve and kill and hate one another? What kind of species *was* this that she'd been born into?

She lowered her head over easily solved geometry problems, then straightened, listening intently. Had she heard tires crunching down the shell driveway? At this hour? In this storm?

"Tony—" she began, but he didn't hear her.

Outside, a car door slammed. Then the door to the living room was thrown open. Standing there, in the rain, was Junie.

18

Junie had always been called, by people who knew her well and by those who hardly knew her at all, a girl. A beautiful, a sloppy, a headstrong, a charming, a feckless—there'd been plenty of adjectives, but the noun had never changed. Junie had been a girl. With lots of long careless dark hair and no clothes sense.

This Junie, who closed the door behind her and stood looking warily at her husband and two of her children, could only be called a woman. Not because her hair was short and trim and shining. Not because she wore her rain-wet clothes stylishly. Taylor couldn't figure out what it was, but Junie didn't look girlish anymore.

Maybe it was that change in her, or maybe just shock, that kept the three of them motionless, staring at her.

"Well—I figured that if you people were going to be down here dodging hurricanes all the time, I'd better come down and dodge them with you."

Jem's book went one way, his cat another, and he was across the room into his mother's arms, hugging her with silent ferocity. In a moment Taylor, too, more slowly, moved to be encircled in the longed-for embrace.

But Tony, getting to his feet, said bitterly, "The season for storms is about over. So you won't be staying long, I take it."

Junie hugged her two older children, released them, pulled her shoes off, walked to the sofa and sat down with a sigh. "It's been such a *long* drive. Rain most of the way and I only stopped once." She got cigarettes from her bag, lit one and looked around, holding the match. "Where are the ashtrays?"

"Grandmother put them away," Jem said. "I'll get you one." Jem, who hated cigarettes as much as Taylor did, looked happy to be doing the errand.

"I'm exhausted," Junie went on. "Wrung right out. *And* hungry. Is there anything to eat, Tony?"

"I'll get you something, Mom," Jem said. He never called her Junie again. "What do you want? We have soup—avocado—or some paté Tony brought back from the restaurant, and there's mango mousse—"

Her eyes traveled over him lovingly. "Oh, how *good* it is to see you. All of you. You just fix me something of everything but not too much of anything, all right, love?" she said to Jem.

"Sure. Sure, I'll fix you something good. Stay right there. I'll be right back." He braked at the kitchen door. "You stay there, Mom. Understand?"

"Don't worry." She smiled at him, then patted the sofa. "Come here beside me, Taylor. We'll sit together until your father's glared out."

"What in hell am I supposed to be doing?" he asked. "Jumping with joy—up and down, like Jem?"

"I thought you might give a little hop."

"Grandstand plays don't delight me. They give me hives."

"This isn't a play. I came back because this is my home. Not this house, necessarily," she said, squeezing Taylor's hand reassuringly. "Florida. The South. I'm not happy up there."

"You weren't happy down here," he reminded her. "You're still running around thinking happiness is the whole shot?"

"Oh, I'll never change my mind about that. I don't know how many people actually achieve it, or how long it lasts if you get it, but yes—happiness is the whole shot."

"I'm still trying to figure this out. You come in out

of the night and the rain, without warning, looking—"

"Yes?" she said, when he stopped. "Looking—what?"

"Okay, okay—you look swell and I like your haircut and so what. What I want to know is what are you doing here? If you're sorry for what you did and want to come back to us, great, that's marvelous—but there're going to be some ground rules laid—"

He blew it, Taylor thought. If she had planned to move right in, and Taylor didn't think that was what her mother had had in mind, but if she had thought of it, Tony had just pushed the absolutely wrong button.

A few weeks away from home had changed Junie in one way for sure. In the old days, if Tony had said such a dumb thing, by now the two of them would've been off on one of their shouting matches. Now Junie smiled. She said, "Tony, I am not sorry for what I did. Maybe sorry for the way I did it. That was bungling. But *leaving*—I had to. It was like struggling up out of the water for air—"

"Melodrama!"

Junie stared at him. After a while she said, "Some things, perhaps, are just not reversible. Maybe this—situation—isn't. But if it were to be, Tony, everyone would have to try to be patient. To understand. To give a little."

Please, Tony, Taylor thought. Please under*stand* what she is saying. She had a feeling he wasn't going to. Maybe he'd been too hurt. Or maybe he was happier—well, happiness wasn't a word you associated with Tony—but maybe he found it easier to live this way. In this orderly house, with his mother keeping the keel even. Everybody didn't have to be happy in the same way. Perhaps peace and order, after all, were Tony's happiness. What it came to was maybe he didn't want her back.

And where does that leave us? she wondered, as Jem came in with a mug of cold avocado soup topped with a swirl of crème fraîche, a paté sandwich on Tony's French bread, coffee in a little white pot with a matching cup, a peach with a kitchen knife to cut it. "I can't find those pretty fruit knives and forks you bought," he said to his mother, putting the tray on the coffee table in front of her, like an offering. "Should I wake up B.J.?"

"Darling, let it wait. He'll knock me down and I won't be able to eat this heavenly food."

Why does she assume that B.J. will knock her down for joy, which is what she means? Taylor thought. How can she be that sure of herself, of her welcome? She was right, of course. B.J. was going to be wild with happiness at the sight of her. No way would he remember how hysterical he'd been at her leaving. Jem was in heaven. And I'm happy, Taylor thought. It's wonderful to have her here, to look at her, be able to touch her—

Only. What happened now?

"You realize," said Tony, "that my mother dropped everything and came down here because we needed her? Because there was a—gap—here and nobody to fill it but her? What about my mother?"

"I'm more grateful to her than I'll ever be able to say. Or allowed to say, probably. Beyond that, what can

I do? Perhaps she'd like to go on living here?"

"I doubt that."

"He's quite right." Grandmother Reddick came into the room. "I heard your voice, June. So distinctive. And so you're back."

"As you see."

How long, Taylor wondered, has she been standing in the dark on the stairway, listening to us? Why does she do things like that?

"You," Grandmother Reddick was saying to Junie, "are incredible. I wonder if you actually comprehend how incredible you are. Having thrown your family into upheaval, removed the props from under your children, caused Tony to lose weight and faith in people— Having disgraced and injured everyone, now you say you've changed your mind?"

"I didn't say that. But if I had, aren't people allowed to change their minds?"

Jem, who'd been happily watching his mother eat, tensed at what she was saying. She glanced at him, and he leaned back in his chair, his expression cautiously relaxing. Jem and Junie had always been able to communicate this way, in silence, with glances. Taylor had never learned the trick. She wanted things at least said, if not spelled out.

"I imagine you can change your mind, no matter what you've done," Grandmother Reddick said stiffly. "If you admit you made a cruel mistake. I suppose you can try to heal the—"

"I don't admit I made a mistake," Junie interrupted.

"And I've never been cruel. Consciously. Maybe in the way I did it, I made a mistake. But at the time I couldn't think. I just had to run."

"Then precisely what are you doing here tonight, if you aren't sorry for what you've done? *If* I may ask."

"You and I, Grandmother Reddick, travel on parallel lines and there's no point trying for communication. But maybe Tony knows what I mean."

"I suppose I do," Tony said slowly. "In a way. I take it we're going to try to learn to know each other? See if there's something to salvage?"

"If you're going to be sarcastic, how can we try to learn anything?"

"I wasn't being sarcastic. I thought I was stating the position."

"Why do you make it sound so hackneyed?"

"It feels hackneyed."

Junie pushed the tray away a little, her supper almost untouched. She lit another cigarette and let out a smoky sigh.

"What I don't understand," said Tony, "is what we're supposed to do right now, tonight. Am I supposed to move into the garage? Are you moving back into the bedroom with me? My mother's using the guest— I mean my mother's in her room—"

"It's all right, Tony. I've never felt like anything *but* a guest," said Grandmother Reddick.

Doesn't that remark border on the cruel? Taylor wondered. Or is it just cruelly honest?

"I'm not staying here!" Junie said loudly. "I'll be staying in Bette Danziger's guest cottage until— For a while."

"You had that arranged before you came down here?" he asked.

"I had to arrange something, didn't I? Or sleep in the garage myself? I was pretty sure you wouldn't be asking me into your bed right away."

"How crude you are," Grandmother Reddick said softly.

"Mother, please," Tony muttered. He moved his head from side to side, as if to ease an ache. "Okay, Junie. I'm willing to give it a shot, if you are."

"Junie! You're here!"

B.J. entered the room shouting, ran to his mother, followed by Drum. The two of them crashed into the coffee table, sending tray and contents flying. Soup and crème fraîche splashed on the new slipcovers, on the rug. The peach rolled across the floor. Drum grabbed the sandwich and gulped it down.

"I'll be in my room," said Grandmother Reddick.

They took her to the airport on Sunday in the late morning. Waiting in line to get her luggage checked through, Grandmother Reddick talked to Tony, who was looking anxious, about her plans for when she got home to Lexington.

"I'll be glad to get back," she said. There was a ring of truth in her voice no one could doubt. "I shall miss the children dreadfully, of course." B.J., sobbing against her skirt, wailed, "Don't go, Granny! Please don't go!" She hugged him, put an arm around Jem's shoulder and said, "You can come to visit me. Wouldn't you like that?"

"I'd love it, Grandmother," said Jem.

"Maybe we could visit when there's snow," said Taylor. She wasn't altogether sure she was included in the invitation, and Grandmother Reddick did not, just now, clear the matter up. She just smiled, handed the man behind the counter her ticket and said, "Nonsmoking section, please, and as far away from those who do smoke as possible."

Watching the bags being ticketed and trundled away, Taylor thought it was peculiar the way airports telescoped time. It seemed that Grandmother Reddick had been with them not for weeks, but for months, for almost ever. But now, as they walked with her to Gate 4 and the flight back to Boston, it seemed as if they were waiting here for her flight from Boston to arrive.

As boarding time approached, Grandmother Reddick at last looked directly at her daughter-in-law. "Well, June, I hope you know what you're doing."

"That's for me and Tony to work out, isn't it?"

"You can try, of course."

"That's what I meant. We can try."

Junie, who despite not ever having much money could still manage to give some pretty swift presents, had offered Grandmother Reddick the Lowestoft tureen. Grandmother Reddick had declined it.

There's no way, Taylor thought, for them ever even to pretend to like each other again, the way they'd pretended in the past. No matter how things worked out between Junie and Tony, all their lives were changed for good. Not, she corrected herself, necessarily for good. Their lives were changed forever by what Junie had done, no matter what had caused her to do it.

Visitors were not allowed in the boarding area, and Grandmother Reddick said she would not in the least mind waiting the few minutes until flight time by herself.

I think she's glad to be by herself again, Taylor thought. Who could blame her? She decided that tonight she would write a letter to Lexington, thanking her grandmother for all she had done. Because she had done so much, and perhaps they hadn't made her understand that they really were grateful.

Kissing each of the children in turn, and then her son, Grandmother Reddick turned to Junie. "Well, good-bye, then."

"Good-bye."

Grandmother hugged her son again, but only when she glanced down at B.J. was there a trace of mist in her eyes. "I'll—I'll see you in Lexington," she said to him. "We'll play Go Fish."

She was gone, into the passenger area, out of sight. Out of our lives? thought Taylor. They wouldn't know if it had come to that for a while yet. She hoped that B.J. and Jem would go to visit her. Maybe she would herself. Maybe.

B.J., tears glistening saltily on his cheeks, beamed at his mother. "Let's go home and go kite flying, huh?" he said. "I'd like to fly some kites."

"Easy come, easy go," said Jem, shaking his head.

"Oh, come on," Taylor said. "He's only four."

Tony and Junie were walking ahead, toward the parking lot. When they got to the station wagon, Tony handed the keys over and said, "Here, you drive."

Junie burst out laughing. She tossed the keys up, caught them and said, "Well, it's a start."

At home they had lunch, then got into bathing suits and biked to the beach to fly kites in a southwest wind. They had five of them arcing and swooping far overhead in a few minutes, then secured the strings with rocks and left them on their own.

The Gulf waters were high and rough, with waves tossing and colliding and tossing gusts and webs of foam.

Taylor wandered away, not far, just enough to be alone, only not altogether alone. Would they, her mother and father, work out a marriage after all? Or would they, as Tony said, give it their best shot, but fail? Junie said she was going to get a job. Part time until B.J. started kindergarten. But she said she wasn't going to be a housekeeper, full time, again.

Tony didn't like it. He'd never liked the idea of Junie's working. But this time he hadn't said anything. You couldn't really tell, listening to them, who was giving in to whom. Who was hoping to outlast the other and win out in the end. It did not, to Taylor, feel like a compromise. It felt like a contest. But maybe, struggling with each other sort of equally, they'd make out better than when Tony had been ruling and Junie furiously giving in?

She watched a bird that at first she took for a gull. But its pattern of flight could not be a gull's. It was swooping, again and again, flying high, then sweeping the beach and mounting again. A hawk. She got her binoculars on him and caught her breath. Long pointed wings, black mustaches. Dark back, pale breast, finely barred tail. He swooped and rose, uttering a sharp ascending cry, then from a great height plunged to take a sanderling in his talons and flew off, still calling. Holding him in her glasses as long as she could, Taylor saw him beat the little bird once with his beak, to kill it. She watched until he was just a spark against the sky.

"I've seen a peregrine falcon," she whispered to herself. She had seen this rare creature, the feathered favorite of medieval kings, flying through today's air with her own eyes. No one was going to believe her, and it didn't matter because she wasn't going to tell anyone. It was as if the falcon had appeared, just at this moment, just for her, because of her great love for all his kind. Pretty soon there would be no peregrine falcons left for anyone to see. The future looked bad for falcons, and it didn't look so good for human beings. But, oh the moments, the glorious moments, to be snatched along the way! Poor little sanderling, she thought. But he'd made a dish for a king.

She wandered back to where the rest of them were building one of their complicated sand castles. It was great, having Junie here. Even Tony, just now, looked alive and joyous. Just the same, she had had her moment of perfect joy and it had nothing to do with them or what they did to her or for her.

MARY STOLZ

One of today's most distinguished and versatile writers, Mary Stolz is the author of more than 40 books that have been enjoyed by millions of young readers. *The New Yorker* calls Mary Stolz "a gifted and intelligent writer, and her books not only re-create for her adolescent readers their complex world but show how their problems and emotional tangles can be solved, or at least accepted." Among her many honors was her nomination for the 1975 National Book Award for her novel *The Edge of Next Year,* and she has had several of her books chosen as ALA Notable Children's Books.

Born in Boston and educated at the Birch Wathen School and Columbia University in New York City, Mary Stolz now lives with her husband, Dr. Thomas C. Jaleski, along the Gulf coast of Florida.

Format by Ellen Weiss
Set in 11/14 Baskerville
Composed by Kingsport Press
Printed by The Book Press
Bound by The Book Press
HARPER & ROW, PUBLISHERS, INC.